MATT PETERS

Pitch Prince

Copyright © 2023 by Matt Peters

All rights reserved. No part of this publication may be reproduced, stored or transmitted in any form or by any means, electronic, mechanical, photocopying, recording, scanning, or otherwise without written permission from the publisher. It is illegal to copy this book, post it to a website, or distribute it by any other means without permission.

This novel is entirely a work of fiction. The names, characters and incidents portrayed in it are the work of the author's imagination. Any resemblance to actual persons, living or dead, events or localities is entirely coincidental.

Matt Peters asserts the moral right to be identified as the author of this work.

First edition

ISBN: 9798375091006

This book was professionally typeset on Reedsy. Find out more at reedsy.com

To Jack, my favourite rugby boy. You made me fall in love with you and then in love with rugby.

Contents

Foreword		iii
1	Chapter One - Rhys	1
2	Chapter Two - Callum	8
3	Chapter Three - Rhys	15
4	Chapter Four - Callum	24
5	Chapter Five - Rhys	34
6	Chapter Six - Callum	41
7	Chapter Seven - Rhys	51
8	Chapter Eight - Callum	60
9	Chapter Nine - Rhys	66
10	Chapter Ten - Callum	76
11	Chapter Eleven - Callum	83
12	Chapter Twelve - Rhys	97
13	Chapter Thirteen - Callum	106
14	Chapter Fourteen - Rhys	109
15	Chapter Fifteen - Callum	124
16	Chapter Sixteen - Rhys	135
17	Chapter Seventeen - Callum	141
18	Chapter Eighteen - Rhys	155
19	Chapter Nineteen - Callum	164
20	Chapter Twenty - Rhys	168
21	Chapter Twenty-One - Callum	171
22	Chapter Twenty-Two - Rhys	176
23	Chapter Twenty-Three - Callum	181

24	Chapter Twenty-Four - Rhys	187
25	Epilogue	194
26	Sneak Peek - Book 2	201
Acknowledgements		209
Also by Matt Peters		210

Foreword

Hi reader.

Just thought I'd let you know before you start reading. There are real locations in this book, and the national teams all exist in some way, shape or form - but the events, characters, club teams and storyline are entirely fictional and come from my imagination. I hope you enjoy.

A little content warning: later in the book, a character uses some pretty dark humour to get through a bad situation. If you'd like, you can skip the last page of Chapter 20 and the first page or so of Chapter 22.

1

Chapter One - Rhys

I took my place in the scrum - right at the back, on the blindside, closest to the edge of the pitch. So close I could hear the individual members of the crowd shouting for us. In a typical play, we wouldn't expect the ball to come this way. I was just the fallback in case play came this way unexpectedly.

Opposite me, Leicester's blindside flanker grinned and winked as he took his place in their scrum. There was no glamour in rugby. Cheek to arse-cheek and hands locked around muddy, slippery thighs.

The Leicester Titans were a formidable team, but we were already one try — five points — ahead of them. If we weren't stuck with our reserve kicker, we'd be another two points up. But it wasn't worth focusing on that now. If Leicester were successful in the scrum they might score to draw level, or pull ahead. And we couldn't have that.

As the referee called for us to crouch I caught the eye of Leicester's number eight at the very back centre of the scrum. Like the flanker opposite he winked. But then he mouthed the word *princess* and I saw red.

I knew rugby was all about rough and tumble, jibes and physicality to rile up the opposition. But I hated it when people used my last name — *Prince* — to feminise me. Since I'd come out, one of the few professional rugby players to do so, it had been used relentlessly by opposition teams. Like my sexuality was some kind of fair game. And it really fucking wasn't. *That number eight better be watching out for me for the rest of the game.*

I locked my eyes on him.

"Bind!" shouted the referee. And we all locked into formation, arms around one another and gripping the backs of shirts, shorts, whatever we could get our hands on.

"Set!" shouted the ref, and the scrum met in the middle with a bang, shoulders straining against shoulder as we each pushed our combined weight toward the opposing team. It was like a practised dance, each team trying to establish dominance over the other in the precious few seconds before Leicester's player fed the ball into the centre of the scrum.

And then it was a desperate scrabble of legs to get the ball before the scrum could collapse under the weight of sixteen men holding themselves up through pure willpower and sweat.

Leicester had found the advantage and the ball made its way back through their ranks and to their number eight. He took a second's hesitation before picking it up and I thought I saw his eyes flicker to my left. It seemed he might come my way then. If he was going to play stupid games, he was going to win stupid prizes. And these big bastards needed to learn that if they were gonna mess with me because I was leaner and shorter than them. Then they'd go down like Goliath.

Rather than pass to the expectant scrum half behind him, number eight feinted right and then ran left. He broke through our quickly forming defensive line like it was nothing, then swerved to avoid me. But I was smaller and faster than the big beardy brute.

I snaked one arm around his thighs as he passed, relying on his own momentum to bring him down. And it did. I felt my own feet leave the floor as he fell, and then all twenty-stone of the bastard landed right on me and pain lanced through me and I heard a pop as my elbow twisted.

I was vaguely aware of the ball being taken from the number eight by a member of his own team, and of him scrambling to his feet like nothing had happened. In rugby, people get lost in the scramble. And I didn't know how long it was before someone finally noticed that I was injured. All I knew was the agony, all I could do was use my good arm to hold on to my bad arm and hope it didn't get trampled.

It felt like the world slowed around me, cheers of the crowd nearest to me dulling to a steady mutter as I waited for the ref to blow the whistle and to stop play.

Our team physios rushed the pitch to attend to me, and both of their faces told me it wasn't good as they painfully poked and prodded at me.

They helped me into a sitting position and I risked a look down. The mottled bruising from wrist to shoulder was most concentrated around my elbow and turning a deep, ugly purple.

"Come on, you're off for the rest of the match...at least," said Bernie, our head physio. He was a young, pretty man of twenty-six who pecked around us like a mother hen with more love and care than I'd ever known from a rugby physio. A quick glance at one of the team medics told me that perhaps he had reason to be worried. They were already looking at me like it was my own funeral.

They escorted me from the pitch as our supporters respectfully clapped me off. As soon as I was to the sidelines, play resumed. I saw a few Leicester Titans stand still without clapping, but there was no booing. And that was the nature of rugby. A barbarian's game played — and supported, for the most part — by gentlemen.

***

The handsome doctor glanced down at my chart before looking back up at me with a wary smile. "Well, you certainly have a tolerance for pain," he said.

"Shall I put that on my Tinder profile?" I asked him. He grimaced back, so it seemed my weak attempt at flirtation had fallen on deaf ears.

"Well, you may need online dating to fill the time over the next couple of months at least. Your arm is going to need quite some time to heal," he said. "You've torn the tendon in your bicep. We'll have you taken in for surgery and book you in for rehabilitation, but you're usually looking at around three months of healing for someone your age. With exercise to get yourself back up to strength, I can see you returning to play in four months or so if you're careful about how you rehabilitate."

"Fuck." It wasn't me who spoke, but my mother. "Are you sure it's that bad?" She was sitting on the side of the fancy private hospital bed, clutching my good hand.

"That's an optimistic prediction, Mrs Prince. Rest assured we'll have Mr Prince up and ready as soon as is possible. If you're willing, we'll have you in surgery in the next few days. There's no reason to delay."

I nodded mutely and the doctor left the room. I hadn't even

CHAPTER ONE - RHYS

bothered getting his name.

"Are you OK, love?" My mum rubbed at my good arm reassuringly as I felt the stupid tears starting to gather at the edge of my eyes.

"I feel…ahh, shit." The tears had started to leak down my face. "I feel like I'm just getting started, I want to…I need to get better. I can't miss out again."

There were so many rugby prodigies in the country. Every generation, a flash new nineteen year old would make it into the Wales squad and take the country by storm. I hadn't been so lucky, playing professional club rugby at a decent level, but never making the national team.

Now twenty four years of age, I had relentlessly pushed and improved. And it was starting to get noticed in the right places, and I knew I had a chance of making the Wales squad for the Autumn Internationals, and the Six Nations. But now that would be tough, if not impossible. I was definitely missing out on the Autumn Internationals as they were less than two months away.

I let the tears fall openly in front of Mum. She had been there for me, always.

"You'll get there, love," she said. "The team will support you."

I couldn't help but feel like I had completely missed out. And that I might never reach my dream. I wanted to be the first openly gay player in the very top flight of rugby union. I wanted to prove the school-yard bullies and the older bastards who still thought I was too weak, that me being gay made me too feminine to play such a rough sport.

It was so difficult, knowing I was on the cusp. Of national team glory. Even if I could just get one minute of International play for the country I'd grown up in, the country that had raised me. I would get better. I knew it. I'd prove them all wrong.

After I'd had just a little cry.

***

A few days later, I was situated back at Mum's house and being waited on hand and foot no matter how much I told her not to bother. That I could do more things with my left hand for now and if I couldn't then I'd have to learn.

But Mum wouldn't have it. She'd always been an awesome single mum, never letting me go without if she could help it. But right now, at home with nothing to do, I was starting to go stir crazy when I couldn't even cook for myself.

"Are you going to let me wipe my own arse?" I quipped as Mum put down a cup of tea in front of me, metal straw poking out like I somehow couldn't pick up the mug with one hand.

"Don't be so bloody sarcastic, I'm looking out for you."

"Sorry Mum." Something familiar caught my eye on the sports channel so I reached over to turn the volume up a little bit. On the screen was Callum Anderson, legend in rugby and all around dreamboat. He was a big, rough guy I'd had the luxury of playing against in club rugby, and it was my dream to play against him in the national red shirt of Wales. They called Callum Anderson the Gentleman of Rugby in the news because he was always so gracious with his opponents, so at odds with the image his body and stern face projected.

That and he was completely, utterly...

"God, that man could do whatever he wanted to me, no questions asked," Mum said, just as entranced as I was with the man on the TV, muddied and ruffled from scrummaging.

CHAPTER ONE - RHYS

"That's gross, Mum."

"Don't pretend you disagree with me, Rhys. I know you had posters of him on the wall when you were a kid."

"Because he was my *idol*." Mum didn't need to know that I still had a poster of him inside the cupboard in my bedroom.

The truth was, my love for Callum Anderson was twofold. Yes, he was incrediblyfuckinghot but also incrediblyfucking straightandmarriedanddevoted. But my admiration for him was mostly in that he was a story I wanted to emulate. A solid starting back for his team, Edinburgh Thistle, but never extraordinary. Until a couple of stellar performances at just the right time, when he was twenty-five, had catapulted him into the national team and rugby stardom.

Now, at thirty-three, Callum wore the captain's armband for the Scottish team and was admired worldwide by rugby fans and by players alike. Like me, he hadn't been the eighteen year old prodigy of rugby we all wanted to be. But through hard work, determination and stubbornness, he had pushed through. And that's what I wanted to do too.

I looked down at my arm, encased in plaster and signed with rude drawings made by immature teammates, and scowled at it. I would get better. I would play for Wales.

2

Chapter Two - Callum

The kids were running around the kitchen islands like loons as my mother in law tapped one manicured hand against the marble. I couldn't stop looking at her nails as they *tap-tap-tapped*. If I asked her to stop she'd only take offence. So I kept my mouth shut and let her carry on with it. Much as it pissed me off. I hadn't long gotten home from training and Elizabeth had been looking after the kids all day.

"Can we go on the Xbox, dad?" asked Logan. I ruffled his strawberry blonde hair, the same colour and wild texture of my own.

"Have you done your homework?" I asked. They both nodded enthusiastically. "Go on then."

"Yay!" both Logan and Olivia ran into the living room. Leaving me alone with Elizabeth. She stared me down.

"Logan is far too soft, Callum."

"What's that supposed to mean?" I asked, biting before I could stop myself.

Elizabeth leaned back in her chair with a smirk. She seemed to take a special kind of pleasure in making people pissed off.

CHAPTER TWO - CALLUM

"What I mean is he's dressed in pink and he has painted nails. He's going to get bullied in school."

I really had to bite my tongue before I responded. Once I'd caused myself enough pain thinking of a considered reply, I finally spoke. "You know Olivia painted his nails under your watch, and there's nothing wrong with a boy wearing pink. The Scottish rugby team's away kit is pink. *I* wear pink."

"Oh I know, that's what I'm worried about." Elizabeth looked at me over narrow glasses. I didn't know what she was insinuating about my masculinity, all six-foot-five of hairy Scottish rugby player — but it raised my hackles, like she'd treaded on something we just didn't talk about. God, I wished my wife would cut her out altogether. But I'd lost a lot of rights in deciding what went on under this roof recently.

"Would you like a cup of tea or were you planning on going straight home?" I asked as diplomatically as possible.

"When is Sarah going to be home? I'd like to see her before I go."

"No idea, I could have her call you when she gets home?"

"Fine." Elizabeth packed her phone into her little handbag. "I'll call Sarah later."

"Lovely as ever to see you," I said to her back as she departed the kitchen. I could hear her saying goodbye to and fussing over the kids, and then she was gone with a click of the front door. I sighed, running my fingers through constantly messy hair before heading to the living room myself to see my kids.

"Dad, Olivia wants to play football but I want to play on the Sims!" Logan whined.

"Well you've got an hour. So you can waste that whole hour arguing or you can play half an hour on football and half an hour on the Sims, " I said. They both immediately turned to the console to play.

I did worry for Logan sometimes, much as Elizabeth's attitude had made me bristly. At eight years old, with his long messy strawberry blonde hair and love for having his nails painted, I worried he was becoming an easy target for bullies in future. But I wasn't going to have Elizabeth bring that attitude into the house. This was his safe place.

Olivia always gave me less worry. She was a typical tomboy, never seen in a skirt or dress and much more likely to be painting her brother's nails with artistic flair than her own. Her teachers liked to say that she might follow in my footsteps. They said she could play for Scotland women's rugby team some day.

I sat on the sofa and watched as they played together on the Xbox. It was much easier than having them run around and trash the house, so I let them have a bit of extra time. Much as Elizabeth's attitude made me want to strangle her sometimes, she had made sure they were washed, fed and had their homework done today so I could have the best bits of being a dad. Just watching my kids be happy.

After Xbox time, I offered to play Monopoly with them to give them some cool down time off the games console before bed. We were halfway through Olivia cleaning Logan and I's bank accounts when the front door opened. A couple of seconds, Sarah stepped into the kitchen.

She was as beautiful as the woman I had married when we were both just twenty-one. Thirteen years later she seemed to have hardly aged a day. Still peroxide blonde with beautiful wide eyes and a figure most women — and men — would kill for. And yet…she gave me a tight smile when she first saw me and then turned all her attention to the kids, who abandoned

CHAPTER TWO - CALLUM

their Monopoly game to tell her all about their school days.

Automatically, I got up to pour her a glass of wine from the fridge. The smile she gave me as she took it from me was much more genuine. "Thanks," she mouthed over Logan's head.

I heated up her dinner in the microwave and let her decompress from her day. "Good day?" I asked as I put the chilli con carne her mother had made down on the counter.

"Alright thank you, very few emergencies. Does feel like we're stretched to our limit now though, we're running out of beds..." she bit her lip worriedly. "Anyway. Not like me to bring the hospital home with me."

"I bring rugby home with me all the time," I smiled.

"Yes, and that's why I'd rather not bring my work home with me too." We both smiled at each other and for just a second I could forget...everything. All the arguments, all the stupid words we couldn't take back, and the one truth that had shattered our marriage open like an egg.

"Are you working tomorrow? Coming to watch the match?" I asked.

"I'm off. Thought I'd take the kids to the park, though. Rather than ask my mother to have them again. Seems a long way to cart the kids all the way down to Cardiff on a Saturday."

"Aye. Of course." I did my best to hide my disappointment that the kids wouldn't be coming to watch. But Sarah hadn't been coming for a while. So it was unfair to ask it of her now, and unfair to ask her to travel.

I looked at the clock. It was only 8pm, but I had to be up early the next day for the short flight down to Cardiff.

"I'm heading to bed, do you want me to take the..." I gestured over to the kids, who had decided that now was the time to empty out Lego onto the kitchen floor.

"No, no worries. They can have a late one," said Sarah. I nodded, headed over to kiss my little ones on the head and wish them goodnight. Then I stretched, poured myself a glass of water from the fancy fridge and headed up the stairs.

The house was big, modern, and paid for mostly by me — though I made sure never to undercut Sarah's work as a nurse. As far as I was concerned, I was massively overpaid for throwing a ball around the field and she was massively underpaid for saving lives as a nurse. This house was my thanks to her and the kids for putting up with me training for weeks at a time, for playing rugby professionally when I should have been playing it in the local park with the kids.

I headed past the kids' bedrooms, past the master bedroom Sarah and I had shared for most of our marriage, and to the spare bedroom at the end of the hallway. It was still bigger than most people's box rooms but sleeping on a small double bed wasn't exactly luxury on my massive frame. Sometimes when I stretched, my toes peeked out from the end of the covers and I yearned for the king-size Sarah and I had shared.

I stripped down to my boxers, climbed into bed and turned on my phone. It had blown up with well-wishes from family and friends after I'd been named in the starting line-up for Edinburgh Thistle, like it wasn't something that happened every week. But it hadn't always been the case so I appreciated the support. I sent back a few thanks and checked Cardiff Old Navy's Instagram to see who was in their starting line up.

Rhys Prince immediately jumped out at me. The young man had injured himself back in October. Now, four months on, it seemed he was already back their line-up.

Something like a pit of dread settled in my stomach even as I hovered over his name, clicking the little tag that would lead

CHAPTER TWO - CALLUM

me to his own personal account.

There were pictures of him playing rugby, out with friends, and — most recently — pictures of the cast on his arm and reassurances to family, fans and friends that he was recovering as quickly as possible. I remembered watching the match where he injured his dominant arm and winced just thinking about the unnatural way his arm had bent, how clear the agony had been on his face before the cameras cut away. I'd thought at the time that could be a career-ending injury for him. To see he was back after just four months was a shock to me, and it seemed it was to everyone else too. There were hundreds of comments under his most recent photo, him training with Cardiff and the announcement that he'd been declared fit to play.

I scrolled idly for a second. I had played against Rhys before, of course. But that was before, when everything seemed easy. Before I had confronted the truth of my own situation.

Before it had all come out in a horrible rush to Sarah and flipped our lives upside down.

Before I had told her I was gay, and effectively ended our marriage then and there.

I felt like a guilty old pervert as I looked through Rhys' account. Just twenty-five and absolutely gorgeous. All that tanned skin and blonde hair that immediately set him apart on any Celtic rugby field, so often filled with stern dark-haired and thick-browed men that looked like they lived and breathed the stuff.

Rhys was...lighter, somehow. Maybe the first in a new breed of players that would take us old timers out altogether. My stomach flipped as I scrolled and stopped at a photo he'd quite clearly taken in the rugby showers. He was holding just his muddy blue rugby shirt to cover any modesty. The rest of him was beautiful golden tanned skin and clearly defined abs. His blonde hair and face were dirtied with mud as were his lower arms and legs, but his smooth chest and stomach were almost dirt-free, planes of sculpted but subtle muscle that screamed fast.

In rugby, there were spaces for people like me, and for people like him. Goliaths and Davids. Tanks and missiles.

I was so jealous of him, so young, with everything ahead of him. Happily, openly gay in the world of rugby. Nothing to hold him back from being whoever he wanted to be. And with those baby blue eyes and that body, as well as his sporting prowess, there was no way the men weren't falling at his feet.

I put my phone away quickly. I didn't need this, not now. I did not need to go down that rabbit-hole. I had to focus on the game and nothing else.

3

Chapter Three - Rhys

It was game day. It was *fucking* game day. And I wanted to scream with excitement. I was finally back in the squad, and being played as a starting player. I was ready to show everyone what it looked like to really come back from the dumps. I'd been staying with my mum for a couple of weeks and commuting into Cardiff because I couldn't bear watching the games from my flat, which overlooked the stadium.

My arm twinged just a tiny bit as I pulled up the handbrake in my car. The doctors had told me that might keep happening for a long time, but my physical assessment had shown a full range of movement and almost full strength. Enough to get me back on the field.

I pulled my kit bag over my shoulder, though it was only my lucky boots and gum-shield. Everything else was in there, waiting for me.

In the Arms Park, the scrappy little stadium that sat literally in the shadow of Wales' Millennium Stadium. That was the most painful thing about playing for Cardiff, sitting in the shadow of the colossus, that mighty 70,000 seat stadium and knowing that stars were made in that place. I had watched so many matches there, imagining my name being called out in Welsh and English by the announcers, feeling pyrotechnic flames scorch my face and the roar of the crowd.

I got out of my car and walked into the player's end of the Arms Park. It was one of the older rugby stadiums in the world and had faced demolition when the bigger and grander Millennium was built. But the owners and team had stood firm, and the Millennium had to adjust its plans to fit the scrappy little place next to it.

I walked into the changing room. The whole team had already gathered and was talking noisily when I got in. A cheer came from somewhere and I waved in its general direction before taking my place next to Finn, an older and wilder player than I who'd been playing for Wales for years. He was as renowned for his antics off the pitch as he was on, legendary for his post match binges and for pulling singers and supermodels. Anyone else with his party attitude would be a liability, but Finn was special. His try-scoring was unmatched and he could push his big bulk through almost any defensive line.

"Feeling better, Princess?" he asked. There was no malice in the insult and he grinned down at me as he stripped off his vest to start getting into kit.

"Worse now I've seen you, Flipper," I replied. He snorted. I started dressing quickly. The room smelled like sport and sweat, and the boys were all chatting absolute crap, but I wouldn't have it any other way. Nowhere was as good a home as this place.

I looked around the room for a second. At six foot, I was actually pretty small for a rugby player. The room was full of big, hulking bastards like the one who had taken me down

CHAPTER THREE - RHYS

and caused me injury. I just had to be more careful about not getting stuck under one of them.

"Right boys, we've got a big game today!" Garrett, our coach had stepped into the room and shouted get our attention. "Some of you..." his eyes swept over me and to Finn, "will want to be playing your best game. Some of Wales' coaching staff will be in attendance and will be watching to see whether you deserve a spot this Six Nations."

I felt a thrill go through the room. We had some regular Wales players — Finn among them — but there was always a chance someone would get picked out of the pack for training with the Welsh squad. I knew after my injury my chances were slim, but that wasn't *none*. I had a chance. I just had to grab it with both hands.

Well, my good hand.

***

We'd already been out on the pitch for training and warm ups but we all took our place in the player tunnel to wait for the announcer to call our names. Some stadiums would have us walking out on the other side of the pitch to the opposition. In the Arms Park, we stood shoulder to shoulder and waited.

Even with only six thousand fans, the Arms Park was a roar from where we stood in the tunnel beneath the crowd.

"Announcing...." The announcer started, and called the Edinburgh visiting team's names out one by one. Fifteen players and eight replacements. As number fifteen, the one player I was most interested in seeing was called out last. I watched as Callum Anderson jogged out in front of me. The crowd clapped politely for each player, with a few shouts from the Scots who had made the long trip down to Cardiff.

I stood in the middle of the line up as the announcer audibly cleared his throat over the microphone. "And now…the home team…Cardiff Navy!"

He called out names in turn, and the crowd went wild as we started our movement toward the pitch. I still felt the same thrill as the very first time he called my name. "And returning…Rhys Prince!"

I felt the hairs on the back of my neck stand up as I jogged out into the brightly floodlit pitch and the crowd went wild. It had started sluicing it down with rain. Perfect rugby weather. It was time to get messy.

The game was scrappy from the start, with us and Edinburgh trading tries and conversions throughout the first half to take us to an even score at half time. I had put in a shift and was panting with exertion and covered in mud as we entered the tunnel, but I hadn't managed to get a try in. We stood in the changing room, shoulders shivering from the cold. Garrett had given a no-nonsense speech about how important it was that we won.

"No shit," muttered Finn to my side. A couple of us laughed and Garrett turned his eyes to us.

"I'd have thought you, Finn, would be most focused on this fucking game so don't give me any of that disrespect. If you want to keep banging supermodels, you better hope you put in a performance that gets you into the Wales squad."

I heard Finn's audible gulp, and Garrett looked at his watch. "Right squad, let's get back out there. Let's show those Scottish wankers what we're fucking made of!"

With a roar, we all ran back out of the changing room and onto the pitch at the same time as Edinburgh's team. There

CHAPTER THREE - RHYS

was a jostle with so many big men in the tiny tunnel and I nudged into Anderson as he exited the tunnel. He shot me a grin and I smiled back. He was a tank and I was an arrow. Let's see what got the most tries.

I was aware that I'd shifted my style of rugby play after my injury. I wasn't as combative, didn't run head first into so many situations. What I did do well was take the ball and run a good distance with it. It got good tackles in but mostly stuck to the sidelines and waited for the ball to come to me. Until I saw Callum Anderson catch the ball and run like a bull down the blindside. There was no one else in a position to tackle him, and I knew he wasn't much faster than me. I strafed to one side so that I could use my left arm to take him down.

It was like he ran in slow motion as I calculated the best angle to tackle him. His skin was like porcelain under the cold floodlights and the sheeting rain had dyed his strawberry hair a darker auburn. I could see the green of his eyes as he got closer. I charged toward his waist and locked around him with my left shoulder, making sure to wrap tight as he came down on top of me. Almost as if shocked that I'd taken him down with my smaller frame, the ball rolled out of his grip and over the touchline.

My shoulder ached but that was par for the course. I'd taken a big guy down without major injury to myself, and got possession of the ball for my team in the process. I'd call that a great success. I got up, dusting myself off and held a hand out to Callum to help him up. He took it and patted me on the back.

"Good tackle," he said. The Gentleman of Rugby.

As the game neared its end, we were just four points behind Edinburgh's score after a couple of penalty kicks and a lucky try had taken them into the lead. With one try, we would win the game. I watched as the clock ticked up steadily toward eighty minutes. It was our turn for a line out throw-in, and if we timed this right we could guarantee success.

I watched as one of my team-mates, Andy, shuffled his feet awkwardly on the sideline as he held the ball and the two teams got into position to attempt a catch. He was delaying just a little bit to run the clock down, and the rest of us stood in line across the pitch in anticipation of the throw.

He threw, and I watched as Finn was thrust up in the air by our team to catch it. After a quick scrabble with an Edinburgh player he had hold of the ball.

The ball got passed backwards along the line with speed, and I was at the very far edge. I ran forward with my team, watching as each player was taken down by the iron-clad Edinburgh defensive before it got passed down the line. I let myself have a really quick glance at the clock. Seventy-nine minutes. If we scored a try now we were guaranteed the win. All I needed to do was support my team...

We approached the halfway line slowly, agonisingly. But then a gap opened up in front of me as Finn took the ball from a downed player. I saw it, and so did he.

I can do this. The ball arced past some of my team-mates and I reached out to grab it without effort. This is when rugby felt as easy as breathing. As soon as the ball was in my grip I tucked it in close to my chest and *ran.* I passed through Edinburgh's defensive line like it was nothing at all, and kept on running. There was only one obstacle in front of me, and it's name was Callum Anderson. I ran as fast as I could as he ran to intercept me, and there was only one thing I could do.

In rugby, one could only be tackled as long as one held the

ball. I couldn't pass forward without getting a yellow card, but I could *kick* forwards. In front of me stood Callum Anderson, behind me and steadily catching up were the other fourteen members of the team.

I dropped the ball and let it connect with my foot, chipping it past Callum and sidestepping him as he realised he couldn't yet touch me. In seconds, he had cottoned on and I could sense him at my rear as I ran for the weird shaped ball. The biggest risk in rugby was never knowing exactly how the ball would roll.

But it was bouncing beautifully toward the try-line, and I dived toward it as it touched that white line, ever conscious of Callum Anderson's laboured breathing behind me. My fingers touched the ball and I applied downward pressure to press it into the grass.

The crowd went wild as I lay there in the grass, panting. I'd sprinted half the pitch with the whole of Edinburgh Thistle in pursuit, and I'd fucking done it. I had won us the game.

Our kicker effortlessly got the ball over the posts and we won the game by three points. The changing-room celebrations were epic, with Finn handing out beers as we all stripped out of the muddy clothes and headed for the showers. Edinburgh would be having a much more sombre discussion in their changing rooms.

I soaped up and washed in the open shower block with no shame. I was the only openly gay member of a professional rugby team in Wales, and not one man on our team gave a shit. Gayer things happened on rugby tours all over the country, but the sport still hadn't ever shed its macho image. I hoped me playing so effortlessly and well for a team like Cardiff meant another kid somewhere out there wasn't afraid of stepping into a changing room.

"Good game there," said Finn as he took his place in the shower next to me. Somehow, he always gravitated towards me. Perhaps because I was young and I thought I'd be a party animal like he was.

I subtly looked at Finn as we showered. Not a gay thing, I knew we all did it. He had a reputation with the ladies, and if rumours were to be believed in some of Cardiff's gay bars then he was active in those too. I could see why. He was tall, broadly muscled from shoulder to ankle and tanned, with close-cropped black hair and caramel-brown eyes. I didn't even need to look downward to know what he was working with.

He'd gained the nickname Flipper from us because of his name, the *Party Player* by the press because of his antics. But in changing rooms, he's gained the nickname *the Horse* for a reason. Something about his wild ways put me off him, and despite us being close I'd never asked him about the bisexuality rumours that flew around Cardiff. If he wanted me —or anyone— to know, he'd talk to me.

"Coming out tonight?" he asked. "I've heard the Edinburgh players are all out at Live Lounge, and I've got priority access."

"Of course you have," I muttered. After a rugby game I liked to decompress in my flat, but it had been so so long since a game. Since I'd scored a try. Since I had been the star of the show. "Fuck it, I'm in. Do you have any…"

"Aftershave, deodorant, toothpaste? Clean shirts? Come check out my stash, I've left no room for people to make excuses not to come out."

Finn brazenly walked out of the showers without grabbing a towel but I wrapped one around my waist before walking out

CHAPTER THREE - RHYS

to join him in the changing room where half the team were now getting dressed in post-match shirt and tie.

"I can't believe you have all this shit," I said, looking into his bulging kit back. There were spare toothbrushes, toiletries and… "Are those condoms?"

"Can never be too careful, brother," said Finn, giving me three.

"Why would I need three?" I asked, tucking them into the pocket of my jeans where they lay folded on the bench.

"Don't tell me you've never had a three-woman…um, man, night," Finn said.

"Are you serious? You think anyone else has the stamina after a match to fuck one person, let alone three?"

"You're missing out, man. The Horse needs feeding."

I punched him on his shoulder. "I don't need to see the fucking horse, so put your clothes on."

"See anyone on the Edinburgh side who takes your fancy? I can run reckon if you want, find out of there are any closeted shirtlifters in the squad…"

This time I whipped him with my towel and he yelped. "Don't say shirt lifters. That's offensive. And isn't that lesbians anyway? And no. I could do without that drama, thanks very much."

"I don't know man, I don't know. You're the expert," he muttered.

4

Chapter Four - Callum

The club was heaving, sweaty and smelly. And so far, at least six different people had asked for my photo and another five had called me a 'Scottish wanker'. The mood had been sombre enough in the team and I wasn't sure if being around a public who'd rather have seen us lose by a much bigger margin was going to help. Rugby was a gentleman's sport but that didn't mean that every fan subscribed to that idea. But dejectedly sitting in the changing room or a quiet hotel bar with a beer wasn't an option for most of the team.

I guessed we all stood out, the average rugby player towering over most club punters and all of us in shirt and tie with the Edinburgh Thistle logo whilst everyone else was in jeans and hoodies. It wasn't the fanciest of clubs and with a live band in the corner playing *Uptown Funk* I couldn't tell if I was way older than the intended market or about a decade younger. The whole place was populated with students and middle aged men with seemingly no in-between.

"Hey!" A shout cut over the loud music from somewhere above. The stairs had been roped off, but at the top stood a big

CHAPTER FOUR - CALLUM

guy I'd played against quite a few times - Finn Roberts from the Cardiff and Wales team. "Come on up!"

I gestured to the rest of the squad and the bouncers let us up. Upstairs was much quieter, much less of a squeeze and gave me less chance of having a drink poured down my white shirt. Every table had a bottle of Prosecco in a bucket in the middle and a tray of shots.

"This is a winner's party!" Finn roared in my face. All I could give back was a tight smile. I was too old for this shit, way too old now. Having kids at twenty-one meant I'd had to mature quick. And clubbing wasn't totally my scene. I just hadn't wanted to be the one member of the team who stayed back at the hotel whilst everyone had a good time.

I looked around at the Wales squad, full of happy faces. All except one. Rhys Prince sat in the corner talking to a girl, and he was gently pushing her away every time she slung an arm over him. Without hesitation I walked straight over and sat in between them. I wasn't a small man so it was a pretty forceful manoeuvre but she seemed to get the message and turned to the player next to her, who was much more receptive to her advances.

"You OK? You looked uncomfortable," I said into his ear.

"All good. Finn likes to invite the ladies up, and they're not for me. They seem to forget that though," Finn replied. I shivered and hoped he wouldn't notice. There he was, putting his sexuality out there like it was nothing. "Any good looking gay boys on your team?" he added.

I had just taken a sip of beer and almost choked. "No," I spluttered. I wasn't about to say anything anytime soon, Sarah and I had agreed, for the kids. And I wasn't exactly good looking, it wasn't like me confessing would do anything for either of us.

"You seem awfully sure," said Rhys. "I can bet you there's at least one closeted player in every team."

"Not in ours," I said too quickly. Far too quickly, as Rhys' eyes narrowed at me in the darkness of the club.

"Never had the Gentleman of Rugby pegged for a homophobe," he said, shifting a tiny bit away from me.

"N-no, I'm not. I promise. Sorry, that sounded wrong."

"Indeed it did." Rhys had turned back to me now but hie eyes were colder. How many horrible men had put him down playing rugby as a gay man?

"I…I really am sorry," I said. "What are you drinking?"

"You don't need to…" he started.

I downed what was left of my bottle of beer. "Seriously. I'm buying myself a drink, what are you having? An apology for my ignorance."

"I'll…come with you. Getting a bit claustrophobic." Rhys looked past me at the long bench seats, which were getting filled gradually with more players from both Edinburgh and Cardiff, as well as a few extra women who had made their way upstairs. We were all sharing rooms so I hoped to god that my hotel room-mate, Steve, wasn't going to bring me back with him. I glanced over, to see two scantily-dressed women clinging to his arms. *Fuck.* I'd sleep in the bathtub if I had to.

We both stood and walked to the bar. Rhys would be relatively tall in any normal situation, at six foot at least. But I towered over him. When another girl approached us, I gently ushered her towards the rugby-player filled corner.

The bar upstairs was much quieter than downstairs. Finn Roberts was chatting to the bartender when we approached, and passed over his credit card to the bartender before turning

CHAPTER FOUR - CALLUM

to us.

"I don't want to know how much all this cost," he said as he gestured to the tables of booze, "but it's good to celebrate a win." He clapped Rhys on one shoulder as he passed and Rhys winced.

"Everything alright with your arm? Surely you weren't playing on an injury." Seemingly on autopilot, I reached out to touch Rhys' bicep gently.

He shrugged away. "Doesn't matter."

I turned to the bartender uneasily. It wasn't nice, or in my nature, to see people hurt. But I hardly knew the man. I pointed to what I wanted and turned to Rhys.

"Same for me, please," he said. I looked at him in the gently pulsing club light. He licked his lips nervously as he stared at the pint being poured by the bartender. No Instagram picture could have prepared me for how mind-blowingly beautiful he was in person. His hair was shiny blonde under the lights and those big blue eyes were wide, pupils blown from the influence of alcohol or the darkness in the room.

Finn Roberts sauntered back over to whisper something in his ear and Rhys laughed and shook his head, batting him away with one friendly hand that rested on his bicep. For just a second I bristled with jealousy before tamping it down. I had a wife and kids at home, and I wasn't going to throw that away in public without giving them time. Much more time.

That still didn't stop my curiosity though. "What was that about?" I asked as I passed him the beer.

"Apparently there's some lads here that wanted to come up... same way as the ladies have come up. For me." I could see he was blushing under the lights.

"Oh, are they?" I asked, my voice on the strained side of

casual.

"Nope," said Rhys. "I'm not one to have my one night stands broadcast over the internet, and you never quite know who you're sleeping with."

"That's…" I struggled to think of a response that didn't sound lame. *Good? Fair? Understandable? I want you?* I settled for just changing the subject instead. "You played really well today. I wouldn't be surprised if we're facing each other in the Six Nations."

"I doubt it," said Rhys. "Not after…this." He gestured with his good arm toward the other. "I'm not playing rugby as combatively. I dodged you well today, but I'm not taking hits like I should. I'm avoiding tackles, I'm avoiding the ball when I really should be getting involved."

"Your evasion did you well today, though," I reasoned, remembering the moment when I thought I might be able to catch him, but he was like a gazelle on the pitch, navigating the mass of bodies with ease.

"It was OK. I got lucky, you might have caught me. Or I might have fucked up the kick. It'll take more than that to get selected by the Welsh squad."

I shook my head. He was obviously a phenomenal player who'd never caught his lucky break. I could see much of my young self in him, but he could do so much better than I ever could. Rhys Prince might just be the future of rugby when I was well beyond my career.

Steve, my room-mate, walked up to us with a girl one each arm. He unlinked his arms from them and leaned in toward me. "I'll be bringing these two back to the hotel with me," he said with a wolfish grin that turned my stomach. "I don't need privacy, and I'm sure they'd be happy to share."

CHAPTER FOUR - CALLUM

"I'm married, Steve," I said through gritted teeth. My frustration might have shown on my face because he backed up quickly.

"No worries, pal. I'll see you later then. If you wouldn't mind staying out for just a couple of hours…"

I gave a jerky nod and he walked down the stairs, gesturing to the two women — no, girls, as they couldn't be much older than twenty — to follow.

"Judging him?" Rhys asked me.

"Is it that obvious?"

"Yes. You have a very expressive face."

I chuckled darkly. "I don't like that rugby has become…this. Like rich footballers getting their rocks off. I was always taught that rugby was for gentlemen. That rugby was a sport for barbarians played by gentlemen. I just don't see that any more."

"Woah, calm down old man. We're not all banging supermodels," said Rhys with a pointed glance at Finn, who was tongue deep in a young woman's mouth. "I'd rather play and go home."

He yawned. "Speaking of, maybe I should call it a night…"

"Please don't go," I said before I could stop myself. God I sounded pathetic. "Steve's left with those two…and I really don't want to go back to my hotel room with all that going on."

"Why not come back to mine?" asked Rhys. My heart skipped a beat, and if his eyes weren't so wide and earnest I might have thought he was coming on to me. But of course he wasn't. He was just being kind.

"N-no, I couldn't."

"Honestly, I've got a sofa bed and I only live down the road. You'll be able to get back to your hotel before anyone notices you're missing."

The thought of getting a few hours' kip before having to head back to whatever mess Steve was making was a welcome thought.

"Let's get out of here then," I said.

"Just gotta tell Finn," he said. "He might be a bit of an animal on the scene but he looks out for me." Rhys headed over to where Finn was snogging and tapped him on the shoulder. I laughed to myself as Finn pulled away from his supermodel-esque conquest and looked blearily at Rhys.

Rhys gestured over to me and Finn's eyes went wide. He asked Rhys a question and Rhys shook his head emphatically, laughing. I felt something coil in my stomach. Had Finn thought we were heading home to sleep *together*?

Rhys walked back over to me and put a hand on my shoulder. I felt like I should physically recoil, put up a barrier between the two of us. But I didn't want him to think I was homophobic. *God*, this was complicated.

"Ready?" he asked. "Got to let any of your teammates where you're going?"

"They'll survive without me," I said. Most of them were deep in conversation with one another or being distracted by a pretty young woman. If our coach found out about any of these antics he'd be giving the whole team a bollocking. I was doing the right thing giving all this a wide berth.

We wrestled through the crowd and walked out into the cold night air, tinged with smoke from late-night revellers. "What time is it?" I asked, looking down at my watch. I couldn't see the face in the dark.

"Fancy Rolex not quite as good as a smartwatch, is it?" Rhys showed me the time on his phone. 11pm.

"I'm getting old," I said.

CHAPTER FOUR - CALLUM

"Think you're getting old? I'm younger by almost a decade and I'm still the one who wanted to leave the club early," Rhys said. "I just can't be arsed with all that any more."

"Me neither," I said. "Not my scene."

"I didn't think so somehow. Come on," Rhys tugged on my arm and I felt that pull in my gut again. What was it? Guilt, shame? Anticipation?

We walked down Cardiff's famous Queen Street together in silence. Surrounded by side-streets and alleyways that led to Cardiff's nightlife, Queen Street was a quiet artery though the city but for the drunken singers and cryers, the homeless sat begging in street corners and the steady noise going out of every McDonald's and Burger King.

"I love this city," said Rhys. "I grew up here, and I know it's not perfect, but it's just..."

"Yeah, I get it," I replied. Though I didn't think it was half as beautiful as Edinburgh, where I'd spent my growing years.

We took a left at the end of the street and I realised we were heading back toward the rugby pitch. "Don't tell me you're living in the fucking stadium."

"Close enough," Rhys chuckled. A couple more alleyways and we were stood outside the block of Victorian buildings just outside the Arms Park.

"You have to be kidding me," I said as Rhys pulled out a key.

"Never, I just really fucking love rugby." He opened the door and gestured for me to head in first. "Fourth floor," he said. The stairwell was dark and I proceeded cautiously up to the fourth floor. Rhys gently pushed me aside and opened up a door at the end of the corridor.

"You know they say you should separate your work and home life," I said.

"Well whoever they are obviously hasn't ever played rugby." Rhys switched lights on in the apartment and it came to life.

It was small, with an open plan living room and kitchen with only one door leading off the apartment.

"Come and take a look," he said, leading me to curtains on one side of the living room. He opened them dramatically to reveal a pair of patio doors that led onto a balcony…that had a view directly of the same rugby pitch on which we had played a game. The floodlights had dimmed but were still on, and beyond the Arms Park I could see the shadow of that great Colossus. The Millennium Stadium.

"Have you ever played there?" I asked, pointing up to one of its towering spires that gave the stadium such a unique look.

"Only a couple of exhibition matches," said Rhys. "It was a dream, but…there were like ten thousand people there. I want to play for Wales. I want that whole place at capacity."

I shivered just at his words. "It's the best venue in the world," I said with reverence. "Murrayfield in Edinburgh might be my home ground, but I've never been awed or scared like I have in the Millennium. When the roof closes, and the Welsh are singing…you'll get there one day, kid."

"Kid?" Rhys snorted. "I appreciate it though, thank you."

He seemed unable to stifle another yawn then, and I saw in the light that he did have dark circles under his eyes. "Tired?" I asked.

"Knackered. I couldn't sleep last night thinking of playing again. Imagine if I did get the chance to play for Wales. I wouldn't sleep for weeks. Right, let's get you to bed."

I smiled gratefully as he pulled the sofa out into a bed and disappeared into the other room before coming back with a duvet and pillows. "Bathroom is through my room," he said, pointing at the door. "So don't worry about disturbing me in the night if you need to go. I sleep like the dead."

"Noted." Rhys walked into his room and switched out the lights on the way, leaving me in darkness but for the dull glow of the floodlights filtering through curtains. I took of my shirt and folded it and my jeans next to the bed. Laying almost naked in Rhys Prince's flat, I let myself wonder for just a second how the hell this had all happened.

5

Chapter Five - Rhys

I woke up in total darkness, just how I liked it. But there was a sliver of light that snaked under my door and told me I was waking up a bit late. Fuck it, I needed the sleep. But then my heart thumped as I remembered that I had someone else sleeping in my flat. A man who I'd fancied from the age of about thirteen. I was just lucky that I'd refused Finn's offers of a few drinks. I might have propositioned the married Gentleman of Rugby if I'd really been drinking.

I got up, pulling on a pair of pyjama bottoms so I wasn't exposing myself to him first thing in the morning, but I didn't bother rooting through drawers for a decent t-shirt. We were rugby players. He'd seen plenty of bare chest in his time.

When I opened the door of my bedroom and stepped out into the living room I was immediately disappointed. The sofa had been folded back in and the bedlinen carefully folded on top of it.

Well. That was disappointing. I'd been hoping to be able to talk to him over a cup of coffee, talk about his long career in rugby and pick his brains on what I could do to better

CHAPTER FIVE - RHYS

Had the Gentleman of Rugby only walked me home out of politeness? I snorted at my own stupidity. He might've been a gentleman, but he certainly wasn't walking me home out of some misguided sense of chivalry. Maybe he just had to get back to the hotel in time for his flight.

I opened up the curtains properly to let the winter sunlight fill the little flat when I saw the note that had been left on the arm of the sofa, a note written with pretty terrible handwriting.

Hi. Sorry I had to leave early. Didn't want to get in trouble with the coach. If you ever want to talk through rugby, or anything else, give me a text.

Beneath the note was a mobile number. I smiled to myself as I put the kettle on to boil and felt my heart flutter in betrayal. *He's straight he's straight he's straight.* My brain's tragic backpedalling didn't do much to stop my heart.

The Gentleman of Rugby had proved himself to be exactly that. Kind, gentle and genuinely thoughtful. And he was *sexy*. I'd known that since I was a kid. I'd seen it in his mud-streaked face on the rugby field. But in the club, walking home, his calm and kind face had been everything. Getting close enough to see the laughter lines on a face that had a good few years to age on me, the patches of stubble that he's missed with a razor. Transplanting that god of the rugby world into real life hadn't made him less attractive, somehow. It had made him *more* attractive. Because now he existed and was real. And I had his number.

And he was straight, with a wife and kids. It was a stupid fantasy to want him and I knew it. I could've gone home with any guy in the club — rugby boys were Kryptonite for gay men as much as they were for women, in my experience — and instead I brought a married father home and had him sleep on my pull-out bed. Real classy.

Still, I reached for my phone after I'd poured myself a strong coffee, any typed just two letters.

Rhys: Hi

* * *

I winced as I lowered myself into the ice bath and then groaned as the icy cold water soaked through the thin fabric of my boxer-briefs.

"Get over yourself," said Finn. He was sitting a couple of metres away in an identical bath and sloshing his legs around like it was nothing.

"It *hurts*," I replied, but lowered myself even further so only my head was showing. Ice baths were horrible and painful but I knew I'd be happier later. Three weeks of solid rugby, both home and away, had battered my body after so much time off. I had bruises on my legs from awkward tackles, a footprint on my chest and that twinge in my arm was still happening on and off.

We were days away from an announcement of the Six Nations squad and I wanted to be fighting fit on the slim chance I got selected. I knew I still wasn't playing aggressive rugby like I should, but I was playing fast, and better than could be expected from my injury.

As Finn let out a groan and stretched his arms above his head, Bernie the physio and Garrett walked in together. I thought I saw Bernie take a step away from Garrett as he registered our presence. "Just…came to check you were both OK," Bernie

CHAPTER FIVE - RHYS

said. "Not drowned, I see. Good. That's good." And then he walked past Garrett and out of the room.

"I'll just…" Garrett pointed over his shoulder and followed Bernie. The normally unflappable coach was bright red.

"Weird," I said.

"Yup…reckon I could get a bird even with my tackle all shrunk from the ice water?" Finn asked after a second.

"Only because your shrunken tackle is still bigger than most of ours before we even get in the water," I muttered back.

"Been looking, have you?" Finn leered at me and I threw an ice cube at his head.

"Shut up," I said.

There was silence for a few moments and I watched as Finn's face twisted downward, as if he was thinking. He seemed to hesitate before opening his mouth which in my experience with him was pretty bloody rare.

"Thing is…" he said, but then my phone rang with no Caller ID, interrupting him. I scrambled out of the icy tub, getting ice all over the floor and slipping on wet tiles before answering.

"Hello?" I said.

"Hi," said a familiar voice down the line - one I had been waiting to hear for years. "Is this a good time to talk?"

"A good-yes, it's a great time to talk. Fire away." I was shivering in just my wet boxers but I needed to hear those magic words.

"Well," said Wesley Peterson, Wales head coach, "I've been very impressed by your performance in the last few weeks and in your quick recovery. Training camp for the Six Nations starts in a week. Are you ready for it?"

"Yes, I am. Thank you so, so mu-" I started, but the line had gone dead.

"You got in?" asked Finn.

I lowered myself back into the tub to still my heart a little. The second dip wasn't as bad as the first.

"I got in," I confirmed. I threw my arms up in the air and screeched as it really hit me. "I got in! Oh my fucking God!"

"I'll request a room with you," said Finn. "Break you in gently."

"As if," I muttered. But smiled to myself. There were a couple of Cardiff Old Navy players in the regular Wales starting line-up, but most of the people there I'd be playing *with* for the first time after years of playing against. I grinned and let myself sink further into the icy water. I better get used to these, there would be many more to come.

I reached for my phone to text my newest friend.

Rhys: I got in.

Callum: No way, that's awesome! I told you you'd do it.

Rhys: Well I wasn't expecting it. So thank you for believing in me.

Callum: Well I look forward to being your worst enemy on the field again.

I snorted reading his message, feeling familiar butterflies attempting to escape my stomach through the cold water.

"Who's got you looking so happy?" Finn asked.

"I'm just happy that I've gotten into the national squad," I replied, letting the phone drop onto the towel next to the bath.

"Have you texted your mum?"

CHAPTER FIVE - RHYS

"Shit!" I reached back down for it and typed out a quick text letting her know. "Done."

"Then who is it you were texting in the first place?" Finn was looking at me quizzically. "Who's the little Prince hiding?"

"No-one!" I said. "No-one. It was just Callum asking whether I'd heard anything."

"Anderson?" Finn asked. "How long have you two been mates?"

"Since he stayed on my sofa," I replied as nonchalantly as was possible.

"Well you better get out of the habit," said Finn. "No friends in international rugby whilst the Six Nations is on."

I laughed at his stupidity and levered myself out of the bath. I'd be getting a call from my mother soon enough, and then the inevitable text and call from every auntie, cousin and random holiday acquaintance I'd ever met.

I bent over to pick up my towel and phone and Finn wolf whistled. "I'd watch out if I were you, Prince."

"What?" I spun, wrapping the towel around my waist.

"Stop wearing thin white boxers in the ice bath. I might not mind seeing your arsehole when you bend over, but it'll shock the other members of the team."

I felt my cheeks flush, and as I walked past him and toward the exit, I pushed his head under the ice with one hand.

"Twat!" he called after me.

"You love it, " I replied, flipping him the middle finger over my shoulder.

***

Camp was *hard*. Really fucking hard. And it was exhilarating.

To wake every morning, head to the gym with some of my heroes, and then to have hours of training and drills outdoors no matter the weather. I felt ready for anything.

There was no guarantee I'd be in the starting line up, or even get a minute of play-time. But it was still my dream to be here. Wesley was a hard-nosed bastard who didn't suffer fools gladly and pushed every single member of the team hard, even those who'd been established parts of the team for years. Even Finn was on his best behaviour, and we were both tucked up in the two twin beds in our room by about ten o'clock every single night.

My muscles were aching, tendons sore and bones weary. But I felt like I was home. In the one place I most wanted to be.

Our first game of the tournament was against Scotland. I was ready. I was ready to pull on the bright red Welsh shirt and do my country proud.

Rhys: We're going to whoop your arses tomorrow.

6

Chapter Six - Callum

I looked down at my phone and laughed to myself.

"What is it?" Sarah asked.

I shook my head. "Just some trash talk from one of the Welsh players."

I replied to Rhys' text quickly.

Callum: I'd like to see you try.

Shit, did that seem suggestive somehow? Had I just sent something completely inappropriate. Did he think I wanted to-

"Callum," said Sarah. "I just asked you who."

"Oh," I replied, eventually dragging myself out of the whole I'd been spiralling into. "Rhys Prince."

"The gay one?" Sarah said. "What a surprise. How long have you had his number then?"

I felt a sliver of guilt twisting up in my gut. "Since the Cardiff match last month."

"And you're just friends, are you?" asked Sarah. Her voice

was low and calm but I could see the hurt in her eyes.

"Yes, we're just friends," I said.

"Have you told him?"

"No."

"Are you going to tell him?"

"Sarah…" I implored, but her eyes met mine and didn't budge. "No. I don't know. It's…hard. I don't know what's safe to say. I don't know what to do."

"You think you don't know what to do? I've been married…" she looked around the kitchen for a moment, but the kids were still asleep upstairs. It was an early Friday morning. I'd been given the Thursday off from Scotland's training camp before our flight up to Cardiff in a couple of hours. "…married to a man who kept part of himself so hidden from me for years. Don't think that now you've told me I won't worry that you're hiding other things from me."

"I just need a friend," I begged. Sarah's eyes softened before she turned to the dishwasher and started loading it with the takeaway plates from the night before. "I just need…since I came out to you, I thought it would be a weight off my shoulders. I thought I'd feel so much better once the secret was out, but now - now we're in separate beds. We live separate lives. You've been my best friend for so long, but of course I don't want to-I can't talk about all this with you."

"So what do you want to do?" Sarah asked. "Who do you want to tell? You've said my parents are off-bounds but now you want some random young kid from Cardiff to know?"

"Tell your bloody parents then!" I realised I'd shouted a little loud and took a seat. "Sorry. I just think we need to talk honestly about our steps forward. About what we do next, as parents to our kids."

CHAPTER SIX - CALLUM

"Are you ready to come out to the papers? To the world?" she asked.

"No," I confessed.

"Then we'll..." I watched her go into what I used to call her *nurse mode*, where she could look at everything logically, juggle it inside her head and then come out with an answer that worked for everyone. "After the Six Nations tournament, we'll talk to the kids and our parents. Tell them we're splitting up, and you can find your own place with a spare room for the kids. They're old enough to decide where they want to go now."

"OK," I said. It was odd to hear her talking so calmly about the breakdown of our marriage.

"And then...only then can you start thinking about *what next*. I don't want the papers speculating that you were shagging men behind my back for our whole marriage. If you want to come out then, or start to go out with men...then we'll talk. But I need you living elsewhere before I can even start to think about having that conversation."

"...thank you." Sarah had given a lot up for me. I couldn't be angry at her for being upset about the end of what had been a very happy and healthy marriage.

I looked down at my phone on the kitchen island. It was almost time to go.

"Am I OK to wake the kids up?" I asked. After two weeks of training camp it was difficult to leave them again. Even knowing I'd be sleeping back at home in the weeks now the initial training camp was over.

Sarah nodded, so I walked up the stairs, past the kit bag waiting by the door. When I had been younger, it had been so exciting to train for two weeks straight with the best Scottish rugby could offer. Now I felt the same excitement, but it was tinged with sadness to be leaving my kids. I always felt like I was missing out.

I crept into Logan's room and gave him a kiss on the forehead. He stirred and reached his arms up to wrap around my shoulders. "Be good for your mum," I said to him. He grumbled something and settled back on the pillow. I pulled the blanket up over his shoulders.

Olivia had fallen asleep and must have left the light on overnight, so I turned it off and pulled up the covers around her before giving her a kiss on the cheek. She was growing up *so fast* and I rarely got much affection from her now, so I savoured moments like this.

When I walked back down the stairs Sarah was waiting by the door for me with kit bag in hand, just like she always had. It would be weird to be losing this ritual along with a lot else when I finally moved out.

"Are you going to be OK with the kids this weekend?" I asked her.

"I've been OK with the kids almost every weekend of the last twelve years," Sarah smiled. I knew she wasn't trying to hurt me with the words, but they stung a little bit. I knew I had to do better.

"Thanks. I'll see you Sunday night," I said.

"You know I'm proud of you, right?" she said. "Despite everything. Despite the fact that we…we couldn't keep things together. I'll always be proud of you when you step out on that pitch."

"Come and watch Italy next week?" I asked. We'd be home at Edinburgh's Murrayfield stadium and were usually guaranteed a win against them.

CHAPTER SIX - CALLUM

"I'll think about it." Sarah thrust the kit bag in my hands. "Now go. You don't want to miss the coach to the airport."

I opened the door, stepping into the early morning chilly March air. It was time to get down to business.

***

Saturday had dawned bright and beautiful in Cardiff. From my hotel on Westgate Street I could see the Millennium Stadium. The funny metal spikes that gave it its iconic appearance pierced the immediate skyline and I could feel the city buzzing with an expectant hum. We were the first kick off of the day at 12 o'clock. Behind me, still laid up in bed, Steve let out a loud fart that ruined the moment.

"Morning," I muttered to him as I stalked past him to the bathroom. I was going to have a word with Feargal, our head coach, about having Steve placed elsewhere for the rest of the away games of the tournament. They had been placing him in my room as he was in the same club team as me, and younger and in need of a guiding hand. In my mind, I already had two kids. I didn't need to shepherd another one who just hadn't grown up in the last twenty-six years of his life. The sooner he got kicked off the squad for doing something stupid the better.

I headed for the shower, locking the door behind me to keep Steve from coming in for any reason, and stripped off. I was amped up for the match already, that old familiar feeling of need to be on the pitch thrumming through every bone. It got me all fired up and I needed a cold shower so I wouldn't just expend all my energy before the game.

I stepped under the spray and let it run through my hair and down my shoulders in rivulets. There was another reason I was feeling so pent up again, and it wasn't just the thought of playing against Wales. It was the thought of playing against Rhys Prince. Since the texts the day before I'd been careful to keep a distance and hadn't sent anything since. But he'd proven to be a phenomenal player in the matches since and had well deserved his selection.

I'd finally bitten the bullet and followed him on Instagram — surely that was allowed — and guiltily scrolled through a couple of times. In the shower, I let my hand drift downward as I thought of some of his most recent posts from Wales' training camp, coming off the pitch muddy and wet with his shirt clinging to his defined chest and biceps.

I was playing with myself under the cool water before I knew it. Rhys was the most beautiful, sexy man I'd ever seen and I knew I wanted him. I'd just successfully kept it under wraps even in my own mind. But now, as I stroked myself lazily under the shower I could imagine what he'd do for me. Would he get on his knees under the cold spray, and swallow my cock down greedily? Or would he expect me to do that for him? Did he want me to fuck him, or for me to bend over, arms against cold tile as he entered me and made me his?

Maybe it all depended on the outcome of the match. Maybe if I won I'd get to decide the terms of engagement, let him impale himself on my cock as further recompense for his team losing the game. Would he moan, scream or stay silent? Was he a gentle lover or fierce? Was-

"Fucking hell, how long are you going to spend in there? I need a shit!" Steve's voice pulled me out of my imagination pretty fucking quickly, and I felt like I'd had a bucket of cold sick thrown over me it was so sudden. What the fuck was I doing? Fantasising about Rhys Prince was only going to be a

CHAPTER SIX - CALLUM

problem later on.

"I'll...I'll be out now," I said. I turned the shower down to the coldest possible setting and let the freezing cold water get rid of my already-softening erection. I had to get Rhys Prince out of my mind before he could affect my game. Or my life.

***

Rhys Prince wasn't playing, or at least he hadn't been for the first sixty-five minutes. But that was changing. The starting number six had been called off and Rhys was coming on to replace him, in his first ever cap for Wales. I could feel a swell of pride for my friend that I tamped down to focus on what was happening. Scotland were winning. Not by a lot, and the game was a hard fought one. But we were winning.

Rhys was like a rocket shoved up the rest of he team's backsides. He was a wonder to watch as soon as he came on to the pitch and I instinctively knew that he'd be captaining the squad some day. He was a natural leader, shouting above the roar of eighty-thousand Welsh fans to perk up the rest of his flagging team. There had been a few substitutions so far but none had claimed the field like Rhys did. I was amazed that he hadn't been called up til now. He should have been on the pitch from the day he turned eighteen.

But the minutes ticked by, and we were at a stalemate. If Scotland could maintain this lead we would be victorious. We just had hold out for another few minutes...but Wales had possession of the ball, and as long as they did they were dangerous.

I was stood slightly back from the defensive line. As number fifteen, I was big and fast and the very last line of defence.

And then I saw him. And he caught the ball. And suddenly, Rhys Prince was the target I needed to take down. One of my teammates reached for him from behind and Rhys twisted out of his grip like an eel and ran through the rest of the defensive line like it was nothing. So it was just me.

In environments like these, the world seemed to fall into slow motion. And all those eighty-thousand fans, their roars faded to nothing. I had one thing in my vision. And that thing was Rhys Prince.

I remembered our conversation in the Cardiff club. He said he wasn't playing aggressively because of his arm injury, seeking out gaps rather than running into tackles. Was that still true? Was it fair to use that against him?

All is fair in love and rugby.

I committed to the tackle, charging him even as he tried to sidestep. But then he was offloading the ball, throwing it to another player I hadn't seen because Rhys Prince was all I saw in my tunnel vision. It was too late for me to stop, and if I tried to pull up now I'd cause even more damage to the both of us.

So our bodies slammed together and I wrapped my arms around his middle. We hit the ground hard, Rhys directly underneath me even as I did my best to stop him from getting too hurt.

The home crowd erupted in a mixture of cheers and boos. Rhys' pass had obviously resulted in a try, and my tackle had looked like vindictive behaviour of the worst kind. It was illegal to tackle a player not in possession of the ball and if I'd been doing my job and looking out for the other player I would have been prepared for the possibility. But I hadn't. Because when he was on the pitch, my eyes could only be on Rhys.

I clambered awkwardly to my feet, pulling my hands out

CHAPTER SIX - CALLUM

from under Rhys to make the task easier. I reached out one hand to help him up, but he glared at me and didn't take it. The second he was on his feet his face was inches from mine, mud splattered and splotchy red with anger.

"What the fuck was that?" he put two hands on my chest and pushed me backward. I was the bigger of us by far but the force surprised me. I took another step back but he kept coming. "Gentleman of rugby trying to foul me is it? Fuck up my arm so that I'm easier to play against next time?"

Before he could continue, teammates from both sides were pulling us back. "What the fuck was that?" asked Lucian, one of our flankers, in his thick Glaswegian accent. "We've lost the fucking game because of your piss-poor tackling."

He was right. Even if they hadn't got the try in, they would have been awarded at the very least a penalty by the referee for my poor tackling. As it was, they'd won by two points even after a poor kick from their kicker. The Millennium Stadium crowd was going wild, but I was just feeling like crap for hurting Rhys. A man I'd really come to see as a friend.

The whole Wales team were celebrating their first match win like loons. I could see them all on the other side of the pitch, arms linked and singing along with the crowd. Every time I caught Rhys' eye, his expression soured before he turned away. I felt worse about that than I did losing the match.

Later in the changing room, where we all sat and spoke like we were at a funeral as we stripped off our kit, and then later in the shower as we washed the grime out of our hair and skin, I couldn't stop thinking of the hurt I'd caused him. I'd gone into the tackle with the aim of winning the game for my country. Well, I'd lost that and the respect of someone I genuinely liked.

Once we were safely back at the hotel and Steve was snoring

in the bed next to me, I reached for my phone to send him a text.

Callum: I really, really am sorry. I didn't mean to hurt you.

7

Chapter Seven - Rhys

Despite the win that should have made us ecstatic, I was in a foul mood. So I'd excused myself from the celebrations at the Cardiff Hilton and walked myself home, hood over my head so that no-one could recognise me in the street. Being mobbed by drunken supporters might have been my dream in a better mood. But not tonight.

The only person I'd told where I was going was Finn, and he'd promised to come and drag me out if the celebrations carried on into town. I doubted Wesley would let that happen so I felt pretty safe in my little flat.

I switched on the sports news, but images of the match and the dirty hit that Callum had gotten on me were the highlights of the night. My attitude afterwards had made some small headlines too, and I my stomach ached as I rubbed one hand over it. I switched over to some Welsh soap opera and browsed my phone. But the algorithm on every social media was shoving the dirty tackle in my face.

I'd read and received Callum's text but hadn't bothered replying. It was obvious that I was going to offload the ball to Alf Thomas to score the try, anyone could have seen that. But apparently he hadn't. And had crashed head-first into my stomach.

After an hour of mindless TV watching and phone browsing I gathered that I was probably safe from Finn attempting to come and get me. So I headed to the bedroom, grabbed a pair of pyjama trousers and got dressed in just those instead. We would be staying at the training camp hotel a few miles away throughout the Six Nations, but nothing was stopping me enjoying my one night by myself.

That night could also include a bit of *me time*, which I'd been sorely missing since we'd been training in such close quarters. It was lucky I was so used to the nudity in the changing rooms because that much male nudity and homoerotic camaraderie could have made stronger-willed men than I hard. Finn enjoyed pulling me and others into the showers butt-naked just a little bit too much for my liking. But that was all part of the lads' rugby experience.

I laid down on my bed and pulled my pyjama bottoms down just a little bit. My cock didn't take much effort to get up, I'd had so much pent up energy and now anger that it was more eager than my brain. I fumbled with one hand on my phone to find something to help me get off, quick and dirty.

I found a video I'd gotten off to hundreds of times, and just as I had started stroking my hard cock there came a knock at my front door.

"Fuck off!" I shouted at…Finn, I presumed, willing myself to get soft. *Think of Margaret Thatcher, think of Margaret Thatcher.*

The next knock came and I pulled up my trousers over my slowly shrinking member. I didn't care, anyway. If Finn saw I had a semi through the thin pyjama fabric, he might have

CHAPTER SEVEN - RHYS

second thoughts about making me go out on the town. *Fuck it.*

A further knock just as I reached the door. "Fucking hell, I'll be there now…"

I stopped as I took in all of Callum Anderson, stood in a hoodie and jeans and holding a bouquet of daffodils. His face was crumpled into a sad frown and his sad green eyes looked big enough to drown in. His eyes drifted down my body, and suddenly I was much more self conscious of what I had just been doing than if it had been Finn at the door. He stepped in close, so close that I could feel the contrast between the warmth of his breath and the cold of the outside rolling off him.

Those eyes drifting downward might have been enough to revive my flagging erection if the next words out of his mouth hadn't been, "I'm so, so sorry Rhys. I would never…I didn't mean…I couldn't hurt you."

And then I realised he wasn't looking at the half-tent in my pyjamas, but at the patchwork of purple that had started to blossom across my abs from the force of his hit. All my anger dissipated at the genuine sorrow in his expression.

One of his big hands reached out from behind the bouquet and brushed against my stomach, at the bruising. It wasn't just the cold that made me shiver.

"Come in," I choked out. "I'll be right back."

As soon as he was inside and the door closed behind him I ran into the bedroom to pull a dressing gown on over my exposed body. I'd never cared about anyone seeing my body before. A combination of grotty changing rooms with prison-style showers and having to grip every part known to man in order to tackle on the field meant I'd managed to lock the *rugby player* part of my brain well away from my *gay man who loves naked men* part. But being exposed in front of Callum had an altogether more intimate feel which I really couldn't let my heart or dick encourage.

When I came back into the main open-plan part of my flat, Callum hadn't moved. He was just stood by the door with those flowers in hand and that sad look on his face.

"Make yourself at home," I said as earnestly as I could. "Beer?"

"No thanks." Callum still hadn't moved.

"Seriously man, you're standing like a statue. Make yourself at home."

I moved past him to the kitchen and put the kettle on to boil. If beer wasn't on the menu, then a good cuppa would have to do.

Finally, I sensed him moving behind me, and I let my shoulders sag in relief as I heard him relax on the sofa. "Milk? Sugar?" I asked.

"Yes please," said Callum. When I was done with the cups of tea, I turned to face him. Callum was sat straight as a rod, still holding the bouquet of daffodils in his hands. He hadn't taken his shoes off either.

"Bloody hell man, get over yourself." Seeing him so cut up was enough to make me completely forget any anger I'd felt toward him. Honestly, it made me want to give him a hug. I put the cups of tea down on the coffee table in front of him and took the flowers from him. I didn't have a vase, so I shoved them in a beer pint glass I had sitting next to the sink and filled it with water.

"Look, I'm really really…" Callum started again.

"Sorry? I know, and it's fine." I took my place on the sofa, leaning in a way that I hoped looked relaxed but made sure I was angled as far away as possible from him. It seemed I'd

CHAPTER SEVEN - RHYS

forgiven him way too easily, but I couldn't let myself sit so close. I reasoned with myself that it was just because I'd had my cock in my hand that I wanted to jump on him. And that distance was doing me good.

"It was a really shitty thing to do, though," said Callum. "I was so completely focused on you that every other rugby instinct just faded away." He seemed to realise what he'd said, and his cold-blotched skin flushed an even deeper shade of red.

"I'll take that as a compliment," I replied. I flashed him my best grin and he flushed even deeper. *Oh my God, I'm flirting with a straight man.* I schooled my face into the best neutral expression I could manage as Callum started talking again.

"I want to be honest…as honest as I can with you, right now Rhys. I don't want to excuse what I did, but I do want to make you understand." He hesitated before carrying on. "Things… aren't great with me right now. I'm facing the breakdown of my marriage, I'm trying to be a good Dad to my kids despite the fact that rugby takes me away for weeks at a time, and I miss them more intensely every single time I go away. I'm trying my best to be a good player too, and, I guess…I guess I fixated on you, a bit. I see a lot of my younger self in you. You're proving yourself at the same rate I did, but you're ten times the player I ever was. I was a little bit jealous of what you've started to carve out for yourself. So when I stood opposite you on that pitch, I saw you. I saw only you."

My stomach did a flip at the words, even though he'd completely explained the context in which he was saying them. Still, other parts of the conversation stuck in my mind. We'd texted about rugby for weeks but never delved very deeply into our personal lives. "You and Sarah…your wife, I mean…you're having troubles?"

"*Had* troubles, past tense," said Callum. "We weren't a perfect couple by any means, but the ending of it is my fault. I decided on the split."

"Why?" I asked before I could stop myself.

"I...I wish I could tell you. It's complicated." Callum's eyes dipped away from mine. Had the Gentleman of Rugby been cheating on his wife? Gambling away their whole life savings? I couldn't imagine the man in front of me ever putting a toe out of line in his marriage. He was the quintessential honourable gentleman of sport in the UK. Everyone had their secrets. But I couldn't fathom a cheater or a liar in those lovely eyes.

It was my turn to look away when he looked back at me. I'd fancied Callum Anderson since I had his posters on my wall as a kid. He had been a figure so far in the distance, unattainable brilliance. And when we'd had internet trouble and porn wouldn't load on my phone, I'd seen the big gruff man on my wall and imagined where those hands might roam when he didn't have them on the rugby ball.

I reached for my tea and took a long slurp until my mind had put itself back into the box. He might have been my childhood hero. He might have gotten even better with age, with laughter lines and traces of grey in his strawberry blonde stubble. But he was my friend now, and he had just spilled his heart out to me. "So, your kids," I said. "You miss them?"

Callum dug out his phone from his pocket and showed it to me. There were two adorable kids on the screen, a taller girl in glasses and a little boy with ginger hair like his father and lipstick smeared around his lips. "Logan and Olivia," he said. "No matter how many Six Nations Grand Slam trophies I have in the cupboard, they are my proudest achievement."

"They look just like you," I said.

CHAPTER SEVEN - RHYS

"God, I hope not."

"How do you cope with missing them?" I asked. "With the Six Nations, Lions and Autumn Internationals this year you must have way less time with them."

Callum looked down at his cup of tea as if it held answers for him. "Can you keep a secret?" he asked, then sighed. "Of course you can. If you can't, I've just told you about the breakdown of my marriage, and fucked that up too." It was odd to hear just how quiet and pensive that thick, deep Scottish brogue of an accent could get. Even when he whispered, it was a rumble.

"It all stays in this flat," I replied. "These four walls hold many secrets."

Callum smiled at me then, and it wasn't forced or fake in any way. It looked a little sad, even, but honest. "I'm giving it all up," he said. "After the British Lions tour, if I even get selected for it."

"You're...giving up what? International rugby?" I asked. I couldn't imagine a world of rugby without Callum Anderson.

"All of it. Edinburgh, the national team. I've made my money, it's time to tell my kids first."

"Do your teams know? Your coaches?" I asked.

Callum laughed quietly. "No one knows. Not even my wife and kids."

That shut me up for a second. "...well, I'm honoured you've told me. You'll be missed in the rugby world. What do you want to do?"

"I don't particularly like my face, but I've been told it's handsome enough to be a pundit. The BBC and a couple of other channels have asked me if I'd ever want to provide commentary. So I guess I will."

"That's...fantastic," I said. I was still reeling from the thought.

But I was glad that he was facing up to what he wanted to do. "Will you miss it?"

"More than anything in the world. Rugby was my first love. But it's taken me until now to realise I need to focus on my other loves."

We went silent then. Would Callum still want to be a friend when the one thing we had in common, playing rugby, was gone? His outpouring made me think that perhaps our friendship was safe no matter what. Or at least, that's what I told myself.

"Fucking hell, look at the time," said Callum. "I've completely outstayed my welcome."

"Never, feel free to call around any time." I meant it.

Callum got up and headed for the door, and I trailed behind him. "Text me so I know you're back to your hotel safe?" I asked.

"Sure. Though I don't think many pissheads in the city centre are going to be a match for me."

"Still," I said, "we're all vulnerable sometimes. Know you don't have to be that big strong man *all* of the time."

Before I knew it, I was being enveloped in a big, tough, bone-crushing hug. I wasn't used to being hugged by people any taller than me, and my forehead rested neatly on his shoulder. His hoodie smelled so at odds with the rugby pitch, light and flowery, and underneath that I could just about make out the smell of Callum himself. A masculine deodorant and the smell of freshly cut grass and earth that seemed to follow so many rugby players no matter how often they showered.

"Thank you for being a friend," he said. And then he was walking down the corridor, down the stairs and away. And I was alone.

CHAPTER SEVEN - RHYS

I shut the door, feeling suddenly quite alone in the tiny flat. Callum had unloaded a lot on me in the time he'd been here, and I wanted to be there for him. Waiting for the text to say he was home safe, I washed and dried out coffee cups and re-arranged the identical daffodils in their makeshift vase three times.

Finally, the text came through.

Callum: Back safe. Thank you for tonight.

I smiled down at my phone and headed to the bedroom. It was late, and I'd have to be up early to get back to the hotel before the coach picked us up to take us back to training camp. Callum's team would be lucky enough to have half the week off and train at their usual spot, Murrayfield Stadium in Edinburgh. Wesley was enough of a hard-arse coach that we would hardly have a day off between games. But Wesley Peterson was a winner. And he gave us winning results.

I shucked my dressing gown off onto the floor and crawled into bed. A problem I'd been ignoring since I got interrupted slowly made itself known, so I let my hand drift down toward it. Without opening my phone again I took my cock in my hand and started to stroke. Just this once, I let the thought of those green eyes looking into mine help me along my way. The thought of Callum Anderson's big hands wrapped around my thighs, pushing them up against my chest as he slowly thrust down into me. The grunts in that beautiful Scottish accent and how he'd sound when he finally unloaded deep inside me.

I came all over my own stomach with a groan to the sound of Callum's voice in my head. *I see you. Only you.*

8

Chapter Eight - Callum

"So, I'm quitting," I said to my expectant audience. My wife and kids were looking at me with completely inscrutable expressions. "If I get selected for the British and Irish Lions tour this year, I'll do it. But after that, there'll be no more rugby. I'll be done."

It was Logan who spoke first. "Does that mean you'll be playing with us more, Daddy?"

I let my face split into the grin that I'd been holding back. *That* was why I was quitting rugby. "Yes, I'll be home much more. I promise."

Both kids rushed to hug me, and I looked at Sarah over their heads. She still hadn't said anything and that worried me.

"That's…great," she finally managed.

"Want an extra hour on the Xbox?" I asked the kids. They both immediately forgot the exciting news I'd just told them and rushed off to the living room before I could change my mind. "Works every time," I said to Sarah. "What's up?"

"It just….everything is changing around us," she said. "I'm constantly wondering where I'll be soon and with you moving

CHAPTER EIGHT - CALLUM

out, giving up the one thing in your life that's lasted longer than our marriage...I just don't know if I know you any more."

I moved in immediately to give her a hug. It was natural, her resting her head on my chest as I pulled her in to reassure her. Easy as breathing.

But it wasn't like the hug that had been replaying in my mind for weeks. The one where Rhys' forehead rested on my shoulder, fitting perfectly between that and my neck like it was meant to be there. The smell of coconut shampoo in his warm blonde hair...

I stepped back from the hug with Sarah. It wasn't fair to her to be thinking of someone else like this. As far as the rest of the world was concerned, we were married, and happily so.

"Are we going to rip the bandage off all at once?" I asked her. "I'll put a notice out in the paper, we'll call our lawyers, I'll move out?"

I had bought the little flat near Murrayfield stadium with my life savings. With no mortgage on our house, Sarah and I had agreed I would give it to her entirely so the kids had a good place to call a family home. And the flat had three bedrooms so the kids would be able to come and stay with me however they liked.

Secretly though, I'd bought the flat because it reminded me of Rhys' place in Cardiff. It was in a squat block of Edwardian buildings, not worlds away from the little place in the Victorian block that Rhys occupied.

"Are you sure you're ready to do this?" Sarah asked.

"I think I have to be. Are you?"

I could see tears pricking at the corner of Sarah's eyes but she gave a weak smile. "Of course. It's only the end of my marriage."

I could feel tears building up inside me too. "I really do love you," I said.

"Just not how I always thought you did," she replied.

"Right."

"We talking to the kids?" she asked.

"Of course."

"Come on then. Let's do it together."

Sarah took my hand and led me to the living room. Where I felt like I was about to break my children's hearts.

***

As it turned out, children were a hell of a lot more resilient than I had ever given them credit for. After a couple of tears and Olivia turning a very clever stare on both of us accompanied by the words "Neither of you cheated, right?" they had taken it in their stride. Both excited to see the new place Daddy would be living in, and asking when they could decorate their new rooms.

I was in bed, scrolling through my phone some hours later. As had become a bit of a habit, I checked Rhys' Instagram. He had posted pictures from his wildly successful Six Nations Tour. Wales had won against every team but England and won the tournament. I had texted him **Shame you can't win everything,** and he had just sent back laughing emojis.

His performances had caused the papers and sports Tik-Tokers to pronounce him *The Welsh Prince of Rugby*, and I'd sent him a couple of texts taking the piss out of his newfound fame. But he deserved the praise. His performance had been phenomenal. One day, he'd captain Wales. And I knew it.

Only once I had been bold enough to text him about anything

CHAPTER EIGHT - CALLUM

actually directly related to my Instagram stalking. He had posted a gym selfie with Finn Roberts, Rhys looking much smaller and sleeker than the bigger, more brutish Finn but still muscular. Almost without thinking, I'd texted:

Callum: Nice gains! Looking great, man.

Rhys: Thanks - you should see how it all looks without the vest.

I had no idea if Rhys knew what he did to me, if he was deliberately pushing boundaries to see what I'd say. Either way, I felt guilty. I'd agreed not to…well, *be gay*, until I moved out. And I wasn't. But I was toeing a very fine line with a man I knew deep down that I was attracted to. I couldn't totally cover it up with laddish language or 'just friends' crap.

I had to get out of this house, out of rugby. Then…maybe then I could make a decision.

Because coming out still scared the crap out of me. I was the Gentleman of Rugby. I had a reputation and honour to uphold. And going out with Sarah, all those years of trying to figure myself out as we got married, had our kids, held each other and made love…to come out now almost felt like more of a failure than not coming out at all. Rhys was young, he had no responsibilities. I had mine. I had a responsibility to my wife and children to not be an embarrassment by making the last twelve years of my life look like a mistake.

I was pulled out of my daydreaming by my phone buzzing in my hand. There was no caller ID. Often, no caller ID meant a sports journalist had found my number. I picked up and put the phone to my ear with some hesitancy. "Hello?"

"Hi Callum, it's Wesley."

Wesley? Peterson? Why was the Welsh Head Coach calling me? I had no Welsh ancestors, and I didn't think anyone would think they could tempt me to play for the Welsh team even if I had. I was Scottish through and through.

"Hi Wesley, what can I do for you?" I asked as diplomatically as possible.

"See, I've been selected as Lions Head Coach this year. How does Captain sound to you?"

What the hell? Captain? Of the British Lions?

The lions tour only ever came around once every four years, and to be chosen for it was the highest honour. The best players from the British nations and Ireland were all desperate to be picked. I'd been on two tours before, but I could never have expected I'd get picked to be captain. Especially when the Head Coach had so many connections to the Welsh team.

"Callum? Are you there?"

"I am…are you sure?" I couldn't believe it. I breathed out, not realising I'd completely stopped breathing for a second.

"Of course I'm fucking sure, did you think I dialled the wrong number?" Wesley's forthright reputation was known worldwide, and I chuckled.

"Not at all. I'd love to. I do have something to tell you though, in case it changes your decision."

"If you've broken your leg in three places you can fuck off." Wesley's voice down the phone was a warning.

"No…I'm going to retire once the tour is done. I don't want you taking me as captain if you think it's going to launch the next few years of my career. If that's alright with you, I'll be honoured."

"Well lad, let's make this a farewell tour for you to remember."

CHAPTER EIGHT - CALLUM

I could almost hear Wesley's smile down the phone. It was almost enough to make me forget all the crap I would have to do first.

9

Chapter Nine - Rhys

I sat with Finn and my mother in the living room of the little flat. It was early May and the patio doors had been flung open. There was a bottle of champagne sitting unopened on the table and we had turned to the sports news.

When I'd asked Finn if he would be watching the Lions selection on the news with his friends or at the local rugby club, he had given a little shrug and said *dunno* with the saddest face in the world. And I realised that the biggest party animal on the Wales squad had no-one to go to when he needed to share a quiet moment. And I realised that perhaps the reason he had gravitated towards me in the first place, the reason he threw so many wild parties, was because he felt alone.

"Can't wait to see your name come up on that screen," I said to him. He just shrugged, but I could see that excitable energy rolling under his skin. I was as thrilled as he was just to watch. I knew the chances of me being picked were slim to none, but I was excited for my friend. And my mum had come along 'just in case' I was selected.

"Are you excited boys?" she asked. She was more amped up

CHAPTER NINE - RHYS

than the two of us and had downed two glasses or white wine in the twenty minutes since we had turned the news on.

My phone buzzed in my pocket just as Mum got up to get another glass.

Callum: Are you watching the Lions selection on TV?

Rhys: Yup. Think you'll still get picked, old man? They might choose you for your ancient wisdom.

Callum: I like your odds ;).

And there it was. A stupid emoji of a winking face that made my heart flutter a little bit. Callum and I had been texting for months, usually daily, just with compliments for the way the other had played or to mention something going on in the rugby world. When the news had broken of his and Sarah's split, I had sent him a commiserating text. But something in the way we were constantly in contact felt different to me.

You're mooning over a straight man who's just divorced his wife, my brain supplied helpfully. I tamped it down and did my best not to think about it until Finn ruined it all of two seconds later.

"Still texting Callum, then?" he asked.

I moved my phone away so that he couldn't see the screen. "Is that any of your business?"

"No need to get offended, boyo. I'm just saying, you're pretty glued to the old man. He's like the Mr Miyagi to your Danny LaRusso."

"Yeah, he is. And you're the Lurch to my Gomez."

Before Finn could shoot back we were interrupted by my

mum's squeal of "ooh, it's starting!" and we turned straight to the TV to watch.

The Lions selection was such a prestigious honour that Wesley wouldn't call anyone but the captain in advance to check availability. The Lions were announced live on TV and if you were selected, you would bloody well go. People missed their kids being born for this kind of stuff.

No wonder he wants to retire. And my brain had already made its way back to Callum. Fucking fantastic.

"So first we have the captain of the squad...and it's Callum Anderson!" the announcer on the TV shouted.

Rhys: You twat. Well done. Can't believe you didn't tell me.

Callum: I was sworn to secrecy :D

"Get off your phone and bloody watch!" said Finn. I put my phone down and hoped that the blush creeping up my face wasn't too obvious.

The announcer read out the names by club. We were expecting thirty or so players overall, and they seemed to be saving the Welsh clubs for last.

"And from Cardiff Old Navy, Finn Roberts!"

"Go on Finn!" I shouted, leaning over to give him a rough hug and clap on the back. I thought I saw him wipe a tear away. I ignored it and reached for the champagne to celebrate his selection. Maybe in four years time, we'd get picked together. If I kept up this level of performance.

"Also from Cardiff Old Navy, Rhys Prince."

My mother screamed. Finn reached over to slap me on the

CHAPTER NINE - RHYS

back. And I just sat there. "What the fuck?" I finally managed.

"You're in, mate!"

"No. I can't be. It must be a mistake." I looked over at my Mum. Surely I couldn't…it wasn't possible. I'd only just made the national squad. Mum's tears were flowing freely as she clutched her glass of wine. "I…did I do it, Mum?"

She nodded through her tears and I felt my heart really ratchet up a gear. I was getting my dream. I was going to New Zealand with the Lions. I couldn't believe it.

I stood up and walked out of the patio doors, looking down onto the Arms Park. The little stadium where it had all begun. I screamed into the air, then, letting it all out. "I'm gonna be a British Lion!"

"And I'm the Queen of England mate, now shut the fuck up!" said a voice from a balcony above. *Right.* Leave it to the Welsh to be brutal in any situation.

Mum joined me on the balcony, closely followed by Finn who handed me a champagne flute. "Welcome to the team, mate," he said.

I grinned at him. This was going to be the best couple of months of my life. My phone buzzed in my pocket.

Callum: Well done, team mate!

Now that was going to be a problem.

***

The training squad had assembled outside the same big hotel we had used last time, to the east of Cardiff and fitted out with all the latest in training equipment. Wesley Peterson had built his legendary rugby empire from here, and Wales had gone from strength to strength on the world stage under his stewardship. The light was dying outside, but Wesley had something to say before we all turned in for the night.

And he stood in front of us all now, Callum Anderson at his side. Callum was wearing a tight fitting tracksuit. He caught my eye and winked. I wanted to melt into the floor right there. Because every time I saw him in the flesh I seemed to feel something stronger for him. And it wasn't just his looks, or how I'd looked up to him for years. It was because he was just as good and great in person, more attractive than any camera could capture and kinder than I could think possible. Months of texting rather than seeing one another in person hadn't left us with any distance between one another. And now we'd be playing in the same team.

He swept one hand through his strawberry blonde hair and messed it up more. I could just about stop myself licking my lips. Fuck. Never meet your heroes. Because you might just want to straddle them.

"So!" Wesley started, breaking me out of the trance I'd been left in by Callum's eyes. "I've gathered you, the best of the best, to take on a monumental task. The All Blacks are one of the very best teams in the world. I know from experience how tough they can bloody be."

Wesley had played against them in his youth and then coached the Wales team through a few unsuccessful matches against the All Blacks. It would give him some poetic justice to win against New Zealand with the Lions Squad.

Wesley continued. "It's going to be bloody hard work, but I want every single one of you to give your all. I want you to make your families proud and your countries proud. Am I

CHAPTER NINE - RHYS

clear, boys?"

"Yes Coach!" we all shouted in unison.

Wesley's smile turned wicked. "Now, I know we'll all be working hard. But we have traditions to hold, don't we?" There were a couple of nervous chuckles through the squad at his words. He gestured to Callum, who leaned down — I definitely was not looking at his arse because I was looking *anywhere* else — and picked up a huge teddy lion from the ground. It was almost the size of him. I groaned, knowing what was coming.

"So, we all know tradition, don't we?" said Callum. "Youngest, least experienced player gets the lion. Bring it with you to the changing rooms, to the pub, everywhere you go. And as we don't have anyone under the age of twenty-five on this tour..." his eyes turned to me.

"Bastard," I muttered as I stepped forward to take the lion from him. He wouldn't let go for a second, leaving me in an awkward tug of war for a lion I very much didn't want to adopt. He smirked as I broke free and walked back to my place amongst the Lions, who were laughing at me. Finn clapped me on the back. I'd already dirtied the lion's tail dragging it back over. I rested it on the top of my suitcase and I felt like its beady eyes were judging me.

"Right! Rooms," said Wesley. "I've put you in with...fuck it, I'm no liar. I've put you in with whoever the fuck I like. We'll be training here for the next two weeks before we head out to New Zealand and you'll be sharing rooms for the month we're out in New Zealand too so you better be fucking used to each other.

Please be Finn, please be Finn, I was chanting in my head. I could make friends with anyone, but the thought of sharing a room with someone who didn't like me, or someone I didn't *quite* gel with filled me with dread. But Finn's name was read early, along with Alfred Thomas. That room would be... interesting given their mutual appreciation for wild partying and wilder women. They would either get along or be so desperate to out-alpha one another that they would be knocking down walls and putting up shelves to prove their masculinity.

I listened as Wesley read out all of the names. I looked around and it seemed like everyone had been accounted for in our little group. Was I being targeted for being the youngest? Would the stuffed lion be my fucking roomie?

"And with the immense pleasure of sharing a room with the captain..." Wesley began, and my heart did a weird little see-saw as it seemed to lift and sink simultaneously. I would be sharing a room with Callum. Probably my best friend aside from Finn on this squad. And yet... I was nervous about it. Nervous because of my growing attraction to him. Because we'd never been in such close contact for so long before. Because I was starting to worry he'd be the one guy I couldn't change in front of without making my attraction very obvious.

Callum looked me in the eye and gave me a wide smile, and I found myself smiling back anyway. It was Callum, my friend. I could do this.

***

Our room was nice, with two double beds and a little kitchenette area as well as a huge walk-in shower room. Because Callum was captain, we'd been placed in the closest room to the training facilities and shower blocks anyway.

CHAPTER NINE - RHYS

And we stood opposite each other, at the ends of our respective beds, each with a suitcase — and me with a stuffed lion that seemed to have a constant judgemental look on its face — and neither of us seemed to have any idea what to say.

"How's...how are things?" I asked.

"Good, good. Things are good," he replied.

OK. "How's Sarah? And the kids?"

"Good. They're good. Really...good," said Callum. "You?"

"Yeah, I'm...good. Sorry to see all the stuff in the news though." The sports press had had a field day speculating over why he and Sarah had split. *Does the Gentleman of Rugby have a SECRET?*

I reached over to my suitcase to start unpacking before Callum spoke again. "Sorry, I don't mean to be...after last time..."

"Callum. We're friends. There's no need for us to be awkward over a heart to heart. I'm glad you spoke to me."

"Really?" he asked. I nodded, and it felt like a little weight had left both of our shoulders. We were friends via text, it couldn't be all that difficult to replace texting with speaking over the next few weeks.

"You going to be OK with being away from the kids for the next six weeks?" I asked.

Callum's face dropped. "Not my favourite thing in the world, but after that then I'm free as a bird. No more rugby. And I get to hang up my hat with bit of pride as Lions captain."

"You're going to be amazing," I said. "Right, let's get unpacked...oh, of course. Of *fucking* course."

"What's wrong?" Callum asked, walking over to my side. I snapped my case shut automatically.

"I left my case with Finn for all of half an hour," I said.

"Literally hardly any time at all and he managed to…"

I opened it slowly so that Callum could see. Over my training kit and other clothes, Finn had packed a layer of shiny condom and lube packets, as well as a massive dildo.

Callum laughed, but when I looked at him he was blushing. I grabbed the dildo and brandished it at him and he leaned back like it was a hot poker.

"Never had you down as a prude," I joked, pushing it further toward him. He took a step further back.

"Not a prude," he said. "Just don't know where it's been."

"Good point. I really hope Finn bought it new…what the fuck am I going to do with all these?" I pointed down at the mass of condoms and lube.

"Start a black market with the other Lions, and keep a tally as to who uses the most…" he said with a grin.

"Gross. I don't even want to know. And the answer is Finn, though I doubt he remembers to use them. Probably about thirty baby Finns running around South Wales."

Callum laughed and filled a glass with water from the kitchen sink.

I took all the offending items and threw them into the bedside drawer, the dildo hardly fitting. "That looks like a challenge," I said without thinking. I heard Callum splutter behind me.

"A challenge?" he said. "That's like a fist!"

"Well someone hasn't been on the kinkier sides of PornHub," I said. Callum went red from neck to ears. "Sorry. Too much?"

"No, no. I've heard worse on rugby tours. It's just weird to hear it from…"

"A gay perspective?" I asked when he tailed off. Callum nodded slowly like he was afraid of offending me, and I smirked

CHAPTER NINE - RHYS

back at him.

"I'm the only gay member of our rugby team," I said to him. "And yet I seem to remember being one of very few not involved in 'arse-shots' a few weeks back. Or when Finn decided that he wanted to judge the foreskin Olympics. And yes, that's as disgusting as it sounds."

Callum laughed. "God, I stay away from all that *lads lads lads* now. Too old."

There was silence for a few minutes as we both unpacked. "Ready for the hardest six weeks of your life?" Callum asked.

"I'm fucking ready," I said.

10

Chapter Ten - Callum

My alarm buzzed for the first day and I rolled over to turn it off. The bed was ridiculously comfortable, warm cotton sheets pulled up to my chest...and I had morning wood. As always. Which wouldn't be a problem if Rhys Prince wasn't already awake, stood in the kitchen in a pair of boxer-briefs which left nothing to the imagination.

Fuck. My. Life. Looking at the smooth globes of his arse, I knew I was living every gay man's dream. And my own worst nightmare. I was achingly hard, I needed to pee and had no way of getting out of bed without him seeing me.

He looked over from where he was filling the kettle with water. "Oh, you're up. Cuppa?

"Yep, I'm up." I was very much up in more than one way than one, but he didn't need to know that. "Are cups of tea your religion or something?"

"I can do you a coffee if you're going to complain," he muttered with a smile.

"No, no. Tea is fine if that's what you're making," I replied. Rhys was somehow better looking in the morning than he was

CHAPTER TEN - CALLUM

in the evening, and I felt jealous as hell. My ginger hair tended to stick at every angle and I felt like a zombie til I'd gotten up and had a shower. His hair was messed up like it had been done for a modelling shoot, and he hummed to himself as he boiled the kettle.

He turned away to fill up the cups, and I sensed my brief window of opportunity. I jumped out of bed and made a run toward the bathroom.

"Woah there Speedy Gonzales," Rhys said, one arm reaching out to snag my own and stopping me in my tracks. "Watch out for the sink in the bathroom, the tap squirts out everywhere…"

He tailed off as he noticed the elephant in the room. For just a second, his eyes honed in on my cock as it strained against my boxer shorts. Then he looked back up into my eyes and I felt for a second like he wanted to say something. His attention was doing nothing to help my morning wood go down, and his hand was still touching my arm. Up close, the smooth plane of Rhys' chest and abs were almost irresistible, and his boxers were cupping the front of him just right…

"Sorry," he finally said, dropping my arm. I didn't think I imagined him glancing back down though.

"It's morning," I grunted in explanation, then ran to the toilet as quickly I could.

I stood over the toilet willing my hard-on to go down, and it took a solid five minutes before I could go back into the main room. Just before I did, I washed my hands and managed to splash myself with the tap that Rhys had warned me about. Not only had he seen my hard in, it now looked like I'd pissed myself. Rhys was still in his boxers and drinking a cup of tea on his bed, the stuffed lion under his head as an extra pillow.

For a second, neither of us spoke. And then Rhys went to

sip his tea and *snorted*.

"What's so funny?" I asked.

"Nothing," he chuckled. "Just don't feel like you have to be freaked out about…all that," he gestured in the vague direction of my groin. "I've seen it all before, we all get morning wood. It's just lucky for me I'm always up before my alarm goes off so you wouldn't have seen me. If we're staying in the same room for six weeks, we're going to see a hell of a lot more of each other than that."

I picked up my tea and sat cross legged on the bed, facing Rhys. His face turned a little more serious at my lack of response.

"I don't want to ask this…" Rhys started, "but you're not ashamed…or shy, or anything…because I'm gay, right?"

"Oh! God no!" I said, way too quickly.

"Good. It's just…there have been times in my life when other rugby players have judged me for it. In the school squad some of the boys asked if they could get changed away from me. When I first joined Cardiff professionally there were enough news articles about it that my mum hid from me…now I'm here, at the pinnacle, I don't want that."

"You being gay doesn't make me uncomfortable in the slightest," I reassured him. It was a lie, but not for the reasons he might think. I took a sip of my tea as I looked at him. All of him. He was so, so beautiful. But it wasn't my place to ask anything of him.

"Also…if you ever do need to, um, take care of that…let me know and I can make myself scarce," Rhys said. "I've shared a room with Finn and walked in on way too many situations that I'd rather not have seen."

I laughed. "I can imagine. He seems to really love the

CHAPTER TEN - CALLUM

nickname 'The Horse', doesn't he? Likes to wave it about a lot."

"Just count yourself lucky you've never woken up with it on your shoulder," Rhys replied. I shuddered. I had a type, and Finn was not it.

My second alarm went off. "Shit, we're going to be late."

I jumped up to get changed, pulling off the boxers I'd spent a day and a night in as Rhys did the same. I couldn't help but glance over at him but we made eye contact and I looked away immediately. So we had both been trying to sneak in a glance. I didn't blame him. We all had at some point. Human nature. Or so I'd always told myself when I was in denial of my sexuality. We both pulled on our tracksuit training kits in silence.

"Wake the fuck up, gay-boy!" came a shout from the corridor followed by a barrage of knocks.

I bristled immediately. "Who the fuck is saying that about you?" I said to Rhys before heading toward the door.

"Leave it!" shouted Rhys just before I could open it. "It was Finn being a knob, no need to go beat anyone up, captain."

"You let him speak to you like that?" I asked.

"Yup," Rhys didn't seem embarrassed at all as he passed me to get to the door. "In rugby, all is fair game when you're on the same team. A little bit of insincere homophobia never hurt me."

As if to prove his point, he opened the door himself to Finn and punched him hard in the arm.

"Ow, what was that for?" asked Finn.

"Ask him," said Rhys, pointing back at me. I gave a tight smile.

***

The week was fucking *gruelling*. If I'd thought that previous Lions training camps were hard, they were nothing compared to the tight ship that Wesley Peterson ran. His idea of a team was more like a machine, where we all would run as cogs within it. All playing and breathing in-sync.

And there were no players as in-sync as Rhys and I, and by some extension, Finn. Finn had reputation for being an amazing player and so did I, but we had never quite clicked in terms of play-style or off field on previous British Lions tours. But with Rhys, we had become a bit of a Golden Trio within the squad. New players weren't often selected to play actual matches against the New Zealand national team, but I thought Wesley would be a fool not to pick Rhys. He brought the whole team together with his charm and playing ability.

I woke one morning towards the end of the first week to Rhys leaving the room in his training gear. I lay back and relaxed. Wesley had *finally* given me a morning off training, so that the rest of the team could train in the case that I, as captain, was injured. The whole team would practice through the morning and I would have that whole time in bed. *Bliss*.

There was one problem that had been niggling at me since day one. A long hard problem that Rhys had seen pretty clearly but that I hadn't been able to revisit since. And now I was guaranteed some time to myself, I thought it might be worth exploring that.

I tossed the sheets off myself and shimmied my boxers down just a little. Rhys had become the worst guilty pleasure of my life in the last week, and every morning I watched him make us our cups of tea in whatever too-tight boxers he'd picked out the night before and did my best not to fucking *drool* over him.

So I let my mind drift to Rhys as I stroked myself slowly and

CHAPTER TEN - CALLUM

leisurely. I may not have been Finn 'The Horse' Roberts but I knew that I had a thick cock, and the thought of Rhys' lips stretched around it made me want to cum instantly. I gripped the base of my cock to stop it from happening. I had all the time in the world to bring myself to climax. I was leaking pre-cum so I used slid one finger over the tip of my cock and brought it to my mouth. I'd never tasted anyone else's cum, and I knew it was something I wanted to explore as soon as I was done with rugby for good.

I stroked myself slowly, letting my eyes close as I imagined Rhys, stretched across the bottom half of the bed with my hand playing through his hair. Would he want me to be gentle with him? Or would he want me to be rough, pushing his head down onto my cock and making him choke? I was new to all this, he could guide me and show me all the things that feel good before I tried them out with him...

And then the door opened. "Sorry, just forgot my..." Rhys looked right at me, between my face and the cock in my hand. He closed the door behind him and we were both frozen in place for a second. I didn't know why I wasn't making a move to cover myself up. I saw *want* in his eyes and for a second, I wanted to invite him over and fulfil my fantasies. And then I realised how much of a fucking stupid idea that was.

I moved my hand slowly from my throbbing cock, so hard it almost hurt, and pulled the covers up around me. Finally, Rhys seemed to unfreeze.

"Gum shield," he said finally. "I forgot my gum shield. Needed it."

And he walked past my bed to his own, grabbed his gum shield from the bedside table and was gone from the room without another look back. I groaned out loud as soon as he was gone. I had royally fucked things up. And yet the thought of his eyes on me was enough to keep me hard. It was time for a cold shower.

11

Chapter Eleven - Callum

We finished training when it was dark and though I'd trained for only half the time the other lads had I was knackered. The next day was Saturday, one week out from a friendly game against Japan, and we were all looking forward to doing sweet fuck all.

"Right boys, to commemorate how well you've all come together...I've put a few grand behind the hotel bar," he said to cheers from the waiting changing room. We were all muddy and freezing but the thought of a few pints was enough to keep us going. We scrambled for the showers as one group, everyone jostling at one another and stripping off at the same time. Despite the secret I was hiding, I'd never found anything erotic or sexy about being around so many naked men. Most of them weren't my type and the shrinkage after a cold day of rugby was enough to make the mightiest of men look tiny under the showers so there was very little to look at there either.

Except for Finn, who was stood under the showers at the opposite end of the block to me, swinging his massive thing round a helicopter to laughs from Rhys. And for some reason, I felt...jealous. Something inside me had claimed Rhys was mine, and I hated seeing him naked next to Finn, and Finn being so comfortably naked with him.

I'm an idiot, I thought as I turned away and started washing myself. *Can't even tell the guy you're gay, let alone that you like the look of him.* So I washed in relative silence and walked past Rhys out of the changing room in my towel. Our room was only metres down the hallway and I was dressed before he got back, wrapped in a towel and laughing at something Finn said before he shut the door in his face.

We looked at one another, me in my shirt and jeans and ready for the night ahead and Rhys wrapped in his towel, hair still damp and dripping onto the laminate floor of the hotel room.

"About earlier..." I started, but Rhys shook his head.

"No worries, seriously. Let's just...not talk about it," he said, his voice strained. I looked away as he got dressed, and when I looked back up he was dressed for the occasion in a floral patterned shirt and jean shorts that hugged his calves.

"You look...nice," I said lamely. He smiled tightly at me. *Fuck.* Had earlier really fucked up our friendship?

"Not so bad yourself," he said. He looked me up and down appraisingly. "For a straight man."

"You wound me," I said. And then he smiled properly and everything felt alright. *Not straight though, are you?* a little part of my brain chimed in, and I crushed it into a tiny little box mentally.

"Ready?" he asked.

"Yep, I'm..." but then my phone started buzzing in my pocket. "Can you wait a sec for me?"

"Of course," Rhys said and perched himself on the edge of

CHAPTER ELEVEN - CALLUM

his bed.

It was a FaceTime call from one of my favourite people. "Hi Olivia, where's your brother?" I asked as her face popped up on the screen."

"Mum made him have a bath. We've been out at the beach *all* day and I'm covered in sand. It's rubbish."

"I thought you liked the beach?"

"God, Dad. I wanted to go to town with my friends. Mum made me come to the beach."

I laughed, and then wondered when she'd become so old. I remembered the days when we couldn't drag her away from us. Now she wanted to spend the days apart. "Did you enjoy though?" I asked.

"It was alright," she said. But I could see her smile light up the screen. Maybe she wasn't too cool for us quite yet.

"Dad! Dad!" Logan pushed into view in a burst of activity and noise. "I caught crabs!"

Rhys snorted and I tried to keep a straight face even as I could see him putting one hand over his mouth to stop him from laughing out loud.

"That's nice mate, where are they now?"

"Mum made me set them all free. I had like four crabs in my bucket all at once! I even cut myself on one of their claws, see!" And he held up his hand in such a way that I had no chance of seeing if there were any cuts as it completely clocked out the camera.

"Well I'm glad you're so happy about your crabs," I said, knowing it would cause Rhys to struggle even further. He let out a snort of laughter and lay back on the bed. I could see a line of smooth tanned skin between his jean shorts and his shirt. I focused back on Logan in the middle of his tirade about the crabs.

"Where's your mum, anyway?" I asked once he'd finished.

"Still cleaning the bath out, it's like the sea in there now! I'm surprised I didn't catch crabs in my swimming trunks, Dad!"

Rhys lost it then, banging his spare hand on the mattress as the other constricted his own mouth to stop noises from coming out. I looked at the time quickly.

"Right kids, Dad's gotta go now. But you be good for your mum and tell her I love you all."

I hung up, and as soon as I put my phone Rhys took his hand away from his face and sucked in a deep breath like he was breathing for the first time in minutes.

"That was too funny," he said as he wiped tears from his eyes.

"Well, kids say stupid things," I said. "Ready?"

"Ready." Callum got up and we headed out of the door and down the corridor to the hotel bar. It had been booked out especially for us, and Finn pulled Rhys into the small group of Welsh players as soon as we got there. Feeling like a bit of a lemon, I sat down next to him rather than with the other Scottish players. *I'm just trying to make sure the teams mix*, I told myself.

"Over here!" Finn waved his hand at someone and I groaned as a pretty waitress brought over a tray piled high with shots, pints and a bottle of very expensive vodka.

"Are you determined to blow all of Wesley's budget on just the Wales table?" I asked him.

"Nah. I'll let the others get a bottle of wine each," he winked. "Though you're Scottish and our captain so I think I've technically been more than generous letting you sit here."

"Twat," Rhys said, cuffing him affectionately on the shoulder. I felt my stomach coil again. The way Finn looked back at

CHAPTER ELEVEN - CALLUM

Rhys…he was interested, I knew it. Maybe it was some kind of closet-case to closet-case gaydar, but Finn Roberts was not straight. I could tell.

And what was stupid was my urge to pull Rhys close to me and claim him as my own. I wanted Finn to back off. I wanted to hold Rhys close and not let a man like Finn anywhere near him. He was stupid, and irresponsible, and reckless and…

"You OK?" Rhys asked, and one warm hand came to rest on my knee. "You were somewhere else for a second there."

"Yeah, uh, fine," I said. I reached for a pint off the table and downed it pretty quickly to distract from my own idiocy.

"Oh we're playing those games now are we?" asked Finn. He grabbed a pint and downed it in seconds.

"No, no, I didn't mean to…" but soon our whole table, and the whole bar full of British and Irish players, were competing to see who could down a pint the fastest. When the glasses were empty, Finn started to challenge some of the English players to shot challenges - first just one shot of whisky, but then quickly mixing up the drinks and drinking the equivalent to three or four shots all at once. I declined the extra shots, and sipped at another pint I'd retrieved for the bar. I was halfway to the table when I realised Rhys didn't have one, and I went back to get him one.

"Hey, is the captain buying pints for everyone now?" Finn asked.

"Just for Rhys…for putting up with me," I said. Rhys grinned at me and clinked his glass with mine in thanks.

"This isn't your scene, is it?" I asked Rhys quietly as Finn got up on the table to sing Tom Jones' Delilah to the whole team. The Welsh players joined in whole-heartedly and the others swallowed their pride for a half-hearted chorus. When they were done, Rhys leaned in.

"Nah, not really. I like a bit of stupidity, but I feel like I'm looking after Finn sometimes so he doesn't get into trouble."

Finn had just bared his big hairy arse to the whole room to a mixture of boos and cheers, and I shuddered.

"He could be one of the greats," I said to Rhys, "but if he does something too stupid in the next couple of years he could fuck it all up."

Rhys nodded. "I know, I've tried telling him."

"Right then boys! Who wants to see me light a shot on fire and drink it?" Finn asked the crowd. People had stopped paying him so much attention but he seemed determined to carry on. I knew I was going to have to stop him. Wesley had deliberately avoided coming down to the bar so he wouldn't have to discipline us for bad behaviour, but there were things that went just that little bit too far and this was one of them.

"Come on, big boy," I said. "Get down off the table and stop being stupid."

Finn looked down at me and I could tell he was already too far gone to care. I couldn't believe he'd gotten so much drink down him in such a short time.

"Who you talking to?" he slurred down at me.

"You, now let's get you down and get some water in you."

Finn jumped down off the table, knocking down some drinks as he did. "You wanna talk to me like that?" he said, squaring up to me. I stood up. He had just a couple of inches in height on me and was more muscular but I knew we'd be even enough in a fight if I fought dirty enough.

Finn stepped closer, then put one hand on my chest, and suddenly Rhys was between us.

"You're being ridiculous Finn," he said. "Get some water in

CHAPTER ELEVEN - CALLUM

you and calm down."

On sight of Rhys, Finn's eyes changed completely. He really did have it bad for the man. Or perhaps their friendship just transcended everything.

"Right, I will….I will calm down. I will…"

And then Finn threw up all over himself, me and Rhys in one motion.

"Oh for fuck's sake!" Rhys pushed Finn backwards into his chair and rushed to the bar to grab a bucket. He was in instant matron mode, holding the bucket under Finn's face as he projectile vomited into it.

"Come on. Room. Now." He hoisted one arm under Finn's armpit and did his best to budge the man but couldn't.

"Help me?" he asked. So I looped one arm around Finn's back and pulled him upright. I retched at the smell of all of us as Rhys deftly kept the bucket under Finn's mouth to catch drips, and we manoeuvred him past baying rugby players and out of the bar door.

"Have you got your key?" Rhys asked. Finn looked at him in confusion and Rhys sighed, digging his hand into Finn's pocket until he found the key card for the room. Rhys opened the door to Finn and Steve's room and we both manoeuvred him in. The smell of sick was gross and the gagging noise Finn was making into the bucket was disgusting.

"For fuck's sake, I can't believe you've gotten into this state on one of the most important tours of your life, man." Rhys said to him. He sat Finn down on the bed and helped him to undress, peeling off the sick-covered clothes and throwing them into a corner.

"Right, let's get you some water," he said. Stupidly I was still jealous of the way he mothered Finn as he lay him back on the bed and got him a glass of water. I just stood there, repulsed by the sick on my clothes. I watched as Rhys expertly tended to Finn and wondered why I was so useless standing back as the younger and less experienced of us did all the work. I was a father, I'd dealt with all this before, but he still seemed to be better at it than me.

After what seemed like an age, Rhys laid out Finn on the bed and put the bucket next to him.

"I think he'll be fine now," he said. "He seems to have stopped being sick."

"…great." I said. I looked down at myself and at Rhys and gave another dry heave.

"Right. Fuck this," said Rhys. He fished under Finn's bed with one arm and pulled out a bottle of whisky. "He owes me this."

"How did you know that was there?" I asked.

"It's Finn. He's always got a stash and he's always predictable," said Rhys. "I won't tell Coach if you don't."

"Fine." I grimaced at him. "But I need a shower first."

"God, me too." Rhys led the way out of Finn's room, checking on him one more time as he left. We walked down the corridor to our room, and Rhys pulled the key card out of his pocket to open the door. When we were in, he swerved over to the kitchen to grab two whisky glasses but then made a beeline for the balcony and I followed him.

By the time I joined him he was already stripping off his shirt and shorts, and he sat at the little table and chair set in just his boxers. I pulled off my own shirt and jeans and threw them into the corner with his. Finally I felt mostly free of the oppressive smell of Finn's mistakes.

Rhys poured a generous measure of whisky and knocked it

CHAPTER ELEVEN - CALLUM

back with ease. I couldn't help but look him over as I grabbed my glass and did the same.

I coughed. "That'll put hairs on your chest, that."

"Is that how you got all yours?" he asked. "Scotch whisky?"

I looked down at my own body. I was a little rough around the edges, with red-orange hair over my chest and stomach and a little bit more body fat than rugby players new to the game were coming in with. A dinosaur at just thirty-three years old.

When I looked up at Rhys, his eyes were more...appraising. Maybe I wasn't as bad looking as I thought.

"Another?" I asked, just to cut through the heavy silence that had fallen between us.

"Please." So I poured another and we both knocked them back.

"Are you going to tell Wesley about Finn?" Rhys asked.

I considered for a second. I had more of a responsibility as captain than I'd ever had before, and I knew that I should be more responsible for people acting up and compromising the team. But Rhys looked so concerned. If only he knew how pliable I was because of those baby blue eyes.

"No," I said. "Not this time. But tomorrow...I'm asking that you talk to him. You need him to know that he can't be like this on Lions tours. I've been with him before and he wasn't this bad. So if there's something that's causing him to act out, or misbehave..."

"I'll talk to him. Thank you. One more?" At my nod, Rhys poured another glass of whisky.

"He likes you, doesn't he?" I asked before taking a swig. Rhys choked on his drink and put it down.

"N-no, I don't think so."

"I see it in the way he looks at you," I said, trying not to let any jealousy creep into my voice. "And it's like…he acts up because of you, like he's showing off. And then when you show disapproval, he calms down straight away."

I finally took a sip of my whisky as Rhys thought. Finally, he spoke. "I hadn't thought of it that way," he said. "But I can see it."

"So you know that he's…" I trailed off. Did he know I was hiding something. Were gaydars actually a universal thing that I'd mostly missed out on?

"I've…heard rumours," Rhys said. "Nothing concrete, and I've never wanted to push his boundaries. He's my friend, and if he wants to tell me something, he can."

I finished my glass of whisky. There was a pleasant buzz running through my body from the alcohol and from sitting outside in the cold with one of my favourite people.

"You know, I'm having a better time talking with you about someone who threw up all over us than I was at the bar with the whole team," I confessed.

"Me too," said Rhys. He held out an empty glass to clink against mine. "Good friends are hard to come by. "

I smiled at him, but then yawned. Whisky could send me to sleep any day. I was a bad Scotsman not being able to handle three drams of whisky.

"I need sleep," I said. "I'm getting old."

Rhys laughed. "Tell me about it. But I need a shower first."

I sniffed myself. "Fucking hell, yeah." We both moved at the same time to stand up and went into the bedroom. Rhys placed the whisky glasses and bottle down on the counter and I walked past him to the bathroom.

"I can't believe you took advantage of my kindness to have a

CHAPTER ELEVEN - CALLUM

shower first," he called after me.

I turned back to face him. Rhys had his hand on one defined hip, and was looking at me in mock-anger. I'd managed to avoid looking at him too much in the darkness of the balcony but he really was beautiful. He was wearing bright blue boxer briefs that packaged him nicely and his body looked more fit and toned than ever after a week of hard training.

I knew from experience that whisky would stop my cock flying at full mast. And I was feeling bold, and stupid. "Want to come in?" I asked. "We've showered enough times together with the team that it's not weird."

Rhys hesitated for a second. "Sure you won't find it strange?" he asked.

"…yeah. I'm sure." I turned my back to him and headed into the bathroom and dropped my pants before turning on the luxurious waterfall shower. I could do this, just showering with a mate. I had done this so many times with so many other rugby players. I stepped under the shower and started washing myself, and only flinched a little when I heard the door close behind me.

He was here. And I felt the disruption of the water flow as Rhys stepped under the flow behind me. I didn't know why I was torturing myself but I turned to face him. We were close enough to touch, but still further away than I was usually from anyone in the confined space of rugby showers. So why did being around Rhys feel so electric?

We both soaped up in silence, avoiding eye contact with one another completely. But every now and then I thought his eyes roved down my body. I did the same, his body looking like it was carved by Michaelangelo as rivulets of water coursed down his chest, through divots in his abs and over a cock that wasn't as big as mine, but looked fucking perfect to me. Where the rest of his body was almost a smooth hairless plane, his cock was surrounded by perfectly trimmed pubes a few shades darker than his blonde hair. As he soaped up his cock, he finally caught my eye.

My cock fought against its usual whisky-imposed exile, and to my horror I started to get hard. Rhys noticed too, and he looked back up at me. We stared at one another for a second. When I finally allowed my eyes to drift downward again, Rhys was hardening too.

Fuck. What could I do? I felt like I'd lured him into the shower under false pretences. But Rhys' hand was tugging at his cock now, not just soaping up. He was deliberately agitating himself in front of me and as I watched we both got to full mast, my cock almost touching his but sitting just above it under the shower water.

He spoke first. "I know you've been…frustrated over the last couple of days. If you want to let it out, that's fine. I…I could do with a release myself."

Almost like he'd given me permission, I reached down to stroke my cock, looking at his as I did so. Fully hard, he'd caught up to me in length. But I was thicker than him by far. Just the sight of him touching himself was enough to make me want to finish, but I stroked slowly, savouring every second. This was my first sexual experience with a man, and if it was my last with Rhys I wanted to make it last.

"Is this OK?" he asked. I nodded silently, not trusting myself to speak. I wanted to touch him, to lean in to kiss him. But that felt strange, and maybe he wouldn't want that. Our hands brushed one another as we both leaned in closer, still stroking ourselves. I matched his rhythm and soon we were both

CHAPTER ELEVEN - CALLUM

breathing heavily, leaning so close I would only have to move an inch to claim his mouth with mine. Our hands brushed each other again, and I laughed nervously. Rhys took his hand off his own cock and brushed against mine again.

"May I?" he asked. I nodded, moving my hand away.

His hands were just a little smaller than mine. His hand clasped around my thicker cock, his thumb and forefinger just about touching as he started to move it up and down my shaft, exposing the pink head of my cock as he did.

"Fuck, Rhys," I said, finally managing to get some words out. I kept my hands to my side, too afraid to touch him. He pushed me out of the direct spray and up against the cold shower wall, one hand on my stomach and the other on my cock.

And then Rhys Prince sank to his knees in front of me. "Let me make your feel good," he said.

I nodded again, and his pretty lips brushed the tip of my cock. I shuddered, holding in a groan. I wanted to put one hand on his head and push him down on to my cock, but I kept them both balled up at my sides to avoid temptation.

He started off gentle, licking and kissing at the very tip as he pulled the foreskin over the head and back again to milk re-cum out of me. And then he got bolder, taking me halfway into his mouth before drawing back again. I noticed one hand drop to his own cock as he kneeled between my legs, and he started wanking himself hard and fast as he started to take me more roughly, drawing almost all of my thick cock into his mouth, gagging and pulling back.

My moans could probably be heard down the corridor but I didn't care, Rhys was bringing me so close to orgasm in the most intense way I'd ever had. I felt my tip touch the back of his throat, and when I looked down at Rhys' lips stretched around my cock, his mouth at the very hilt, I lost it.

"Fuck, I'm going to…"

Rhys pulled off my cock smoothly, using one hand to stroke me as he did the same with his, getting faster and faster on both of our cocks until we were both moaning and spilling in unison. He angled my cock toward his chest and his own upwards so that he was covered in both of our releases. My load was a week coming, and I watched as it coated him. I had never been so turned on in my life.

For just a second, life was serenity. I looked down at the most beautiful man I'd ever known and he looked up at me, and I thought I would want this for the rest of my life.

And then Rhys' expression became inscrutable. He stood quickly, grabbing the shampoo and washing the evidence off his body and down the drain.

"Thanks, I needed that," he said. And then he left the bathroom without another word.

Well, I thought. *This could get awkward.*

Chapter Twelve - Rhys

I tossed and turned all night, memory of the night before burrowing into the deepest recesses of my mind and guilt flipping my psyche in every direction. Every time I turned in the direction of Callum's bed, I would catch sight of his head turned away in the bed and want to disappear in shame.

Did I take advantage? We had both been drinking, and Callum had invited me in to the shower. It just felt a little like I'd taken advantage of our closeness, of his body's natural reaction to the amount of pent-up sexual frustration we had. Not to mention that as far as I was aware, Callum was straight. And what had happened didn't change that in any way. I'd been with plenty of men who called themselves straight, and were just looking for a hole to fill. And that was fine, if he was. I had provided…a service, at the end of the day.

But my bloody heart wouldn't listen. Because Callum was my friend. And he was beautiful. And I wanted to be his friend, or I wanted to be more. And I couldn't just be a one time hookup.

Fuck. I had taken something non-complicated and completely and utterly over-complicated it to a point of stupidity. And when Callum woke in the morning our relationship would have entirely changed for the worse. A straight man, a mentor I looked up to and one of my best friends would forever associate me with getting on my knees for a quick release.

Eventually the sun rose, and I knew there was no way I was getting back to sleep. Callum snored lightly, and had turned toward me in the night. If I wasn't going to be waking up next to him in the morning then I didn't want him. I shouldn't have propositioned him without thinking about what could come next.

My phone buzzed on the bedside table. It was a message from Finn that simply read **Fuck. My. Life.** I text him back asking to meet outside his room in five minutes, and he sent back a thumbs-up emoji.

I got up and got dressed as quietly as possible. Callum slept like the dead but I didn't want to risk an awkward conversation. Not yet.

Finn was waiting for me outside his bedroom in the corridor, face grey and expression glum.

"Cheer up, it might never happen," I said to him. After the night I'd had it was fucking wonderful to see someone feeling so much worse.

"Piss off," he replied.

"Let's go get you fixed up," I said. We walked together to the hotel's cafe in silence, each of us got a coffee to take away and walked out onto the hotel grounds. The hotel was surrounded by lush fields and golf courses so we walked over a little stream, far from the hotel and prying ears before we could start talking.

"So," I started. Finn cut across before I could say any more.

"I fucked up, didn't I?" Finn said. "I remember getting up

CHAPTER TWELVE - RHYS

on the table, and then there's…not much. But my clothes are covered and the whole room smelled like puke. I've no idea how Alf managed to get in and sleep there because it's fucking disgusting."

"Yeah, bud. It wasn't good." I explained in detail the events of the night before and Finn seemed to sink lower and lower as I spoke.

"Fucking hell, I really pushed my limits."

"I think you broke past any limits, if I'm honest. You were a fucking mess."

"Did I drink all my whisky too? It's not under my bed any more."

I considered lying but decided against it. "Nah, I took it as payment for all the sick Callum and I are gonna have to get out of our clothes."

"Gross. Sorry again."

"Why, Finn?" I finally asked. We had reached the top of a small hill on the golf course, and I sat down. I patted the ground next to me and Finn sat next to me. He stank of booze. "Why do you have the be the most drunk at every occasion? Be the biggest personality, the centre of attention no matter how bad?"

"I…I dunno," Finn said. "Would you believe me if I said I'm deeper than I look? Like, I'm not just the big boneheaded alcoholic everyone seems to think I am. I…I have issues."

"Do you want to talk about them?" I asked.

"I dunno, man. There's stuff I haven't told myself yet, let alone said out loud." Finn stood up, pacing with the coffee cup and blocking out the sun as he passed in front of my face. "How… how did you know you were definitely gay?"

Ah. So we were finally going down that route. "Honestly?

Porn," I said. "When I was like thirteen or fourteen and all my mates were watching lesbian porn, I was…not. And then I grew older and realised it wasn't a phase. And then the boys that I experimented with grew out of it and I didn't, and then I knew it wasn't just a phase."

"So…say I slept with women, yeah? And it was great. But then a couple of times, after a lot to drink, I slept with some men. And I…kinda liked it, right? What would that make me?"

I chuckled. "God, you're starting to sound like a Reddit post. But you could be bi, or pan, or anything else. You might just like men in bed, or you might like them emotionally too."

"And what if I did like a particular guy?" Finn was frantic now, pacing at a speed that would have me hurling if I was as hungover as him.

I see it in the way he looks at you, Callum had said. I had to ask. "It's not me, is it?"

"God no. No. No way. You're way too fit," Finn said.

"…thank you?"

"No, I mean…so there's someone I think, looking back, I liked. And at the time, I was so confused about all this that he passed me by."

"So you're telling me you drink and act out because you fancied someone once and didn't tell them?" I asked. "We've all been there, mate. But there's a time where you have to stop."

"No, no. I drink…I think I drink because it makes me brave. Drunk Finn tries new things. I'm like…someone else after a drink."

"That's not always a good thing, mate." I gestured for him to sit back down and I put an arm around him.

He leaned into the touch and I did my best not to flinch at the smell of alcohol. "Callum said he won't tell on you to Wesley,

CHAPTER TWELVE - RHYS

but I don't know if someone else will. We were all there to get drunk and have a good time, but you took the piss. You pushed the line so far it no longer exists."

"I know. I'm sorry."

"It's not me you should be apologising to. In fact, I don't think you need to kiss anyone's arse except for Wesley's if he finds out. But you need to have a look at yourself. You're building a reputation for yourself that'll make things more difficult for you in future."

"I know, man. I know." Finn smiled weakly at me. The coffee seemed to have injected just a little bit of life into him. "How was your night? Did you and Callum head back out afterwards?"

I felt the blush creeping up my neck and my ears burned. "Nah. Just a quiet one in."

"Oh my God, you fancy him don't you?" Finn smiled and jabbed me on the shoulder when I didn't reply.

"We came out here to discuss your problems, not mine." I got up and Finn followed way too quickly as I crossed the golf course.

"Well we can multi-task," said Finn. "How long have you wanted to fuck the great Callum Anderson?"

"Since I was about fifteen, as did every gay boy who's ever been into rugby men," I deflected.

"Sure, sure. Does he know?"

"Of course he doesn't, he's straight," I said. Whatever Finn had confessed to me it wasn't my place to say what had happened the night before.

"So is spaghetti till it gets wet," said Finn. Imagining what had happened when Callum and I got wet had my face heating up so quickly that the redness may well have been visible from space. "Oh my God, you really do fancy him. Tough luck man."

"I know," I muttered. No use hiding it from Finn. I'd led us back to the little stream that separate the golf course from the hotel. "Finn…just know anything you say to me is sacred, is safe. I'm here for you. And I want you to get better."

"I'm already better," said Finn. He leaned in for a hug but then veered away at the last second, and started to throw up right into the picturesque stream.

"Sure thing. Come on, let's get you breakfast."

Finn wiped at his mouth with his sleeve and nodded.

The hotel restaurant was full of slightly hungover players from the night before. I nodded at a few in greeting and some of them nodded back. Others regarded Finn warily like he'd personally infected them with alcoholism. We sat down on an empty table for two and ordered from a friendly waitress. Each of us had a Full English piled with everything available on the menu. Grease was a kill or cure for a bad hangover and Finn struggled to get the first few bites down.

I looked up as I heard raised voices on the other side of the room. Steve Ford, one of Callum's rugby team-mates and one of the few men who could match Finn drink for drink, had stormed in and Callum was following him. "You better watch your back, Steve," he was saying.

"Is that a threat?" Steve's voice carried across the restaurant.

"Not a threat," said Callum calmly. "But you better not put a foot wrong throughout this tour, I swear to God. Those in glass houses shouldn't throw stones and your from what I know about you, your house is made of especially thin fucking glass."

Steve went pale and pushed past Callum out of the restaurant, apparently no longer interested in his food. Callum scanned

CHAPTER TWELVE - RHYS

the restaurant and his eyes finally settled on us. I felt something ugly and painful coil in my gut at his gaze. He looked furious.

He walked over to us with a stiffness in his gait I'd never seen before. What the fuck had he been arguing with Steve about?

"Come with me," he said to both of us. "I'm sorry to do this now, but just come with me."

We both stood immediately and followed him out. Callum led us both to the room I shared with Callum and closed the door. His face didn't once budge from the frown that seemed deep-set in it now.

With the door closed, Callum finally exploded. "Steve fucking told Wesley. About last night."

For a second, I thought he meant about us. But Callum's eyes were firmly fixed on Finn. "Fuck," I said when Finn didn't respond. Finn looked grey again and I moved to sit him down on the bed. "Fuck, fuck, fuck. What does this mean?"

"It means that Finn and I are in major fucking trouble. I'm the captain, I should have told Wesley immediately. And Finn should never have been in that kind of state in the first place. It threatens the team's cohesion and our reputation if it gets out."

"So…what does this mean for you and Finn?" I asked. "Are you going to get a bollocking?"

"At least. It's made it worse that I didn't talk to Wesley myself. Maybe I should…"

"Go on," I said. "Go and talk to him now. I'll look after Finn here."

"Steve better not put a toe out of line," said Callum as he headed for the door. "That man has enough skeletons in his closet that could come out if he's not careful. He's hardly an example of fucking propriety."

Finn and I were left alone in the room as the door closed.

"Shit," he finally said.

"Shit indeed."

"Do you think I'll get kicked off the team?" he asked. Finn looked up at me and for the first time since I'd known him I thought I saw tears in his eyes.

I could have lied to him to make him feel better. But with Wesley's reputation for bluntness that lie would be blown out of the water pretty quickly. "I don't know, bud. You fucked up pretty bad this time."

Finn looked down to hide his face, and I could see his shoulders shaking. "C'mere, mate," I said. I sat down next to him and reached an arm around him. He sobbed into my shoulder for a solid five minutes as I did my best to console him.

Callum knocked before walking back into the room. Finn jerked away from me as if afraid of showing any sign of weakness but with his red, puffy eyes and tear streaked cheeks and the soaked shoulder of my t-shirt it wasn't the most convincing of things.

Callum sighed and shook his head gently. "Finn, Wesley... wants to talk to you. I'm sorry mate."

I stood up at the same time as Finn but he held out one arm to stop me. "I've got to do this myself. I'm not having you mixed up in this crap too, and I need to start taking responsibility for myself." He gave me one watery smile before the door closed behind him.

"Fucking hell," I put my head into my hands, rubbing at my eyes to clear the beginnings of any tears. Callum sat down beside me and rubbed my back with one of his hands.

"How you feeling?" he asked.

CHAPTER TWELVE - RHYS

"Shit. How are you? What did Wesley say?"

"I clung onto my captaincy by the skin of my teeth, he's angry I didn't report it to him immediately. I made sure you weren't implicated but...Finn crossed a line. There's no coming back from what he did, especially with a player complaint from Steve."

"Is it rubbish that I'm glad?" I asked, sounding horrible at the sound of my own question. "Not glad that Finn is gone, that's...awful. But it was a long time coming. I didn't want you going too. You're my best friend on this tour."

Callum squeezed my side and I felt a shiver run through my whole body. I thought he might have noticed too. "About last night..."

"Stupid mistake," I cut in. I didn't want the embarrassment of the *I'm straight, I can't do this, please don't tell anyone* I'd had so many times in the ultra macho rugby environment. "Forget about it. We both needed some kind of relief, we both got it. No need to dwell."

"Well, yes, but..." he started, but I cut him off again.

"Seriously, Callum. Talking about it...won't help. I don't want to keep thinking about it, and I don't want to effect our friendship. Because that's the one thing on this tour I cannot lose after losing Finn."

"OK," said Callum. His hand snaked around my shoulder and pulled me in closer to him. So close we could kiss if we wanted to. But the only thing more devastating than a rejection now would be a rejection later. So I laid on his shoulder and let the tears leak out slowly for Finn.

13

Chapter Thirteen - Callum

How could I solve a problem like Rhys Prince? The man was starting to take up more and more of my waking hours, and it was getting harder to deny to myself or to him that I had feelings, both physical and emotional, for him. Since the night we'd showered together and the day of Finn's unceremonious departure from the Lions we hadn't spoken about what happened. And Finn seemed just fine with that.

Me? I was not fine with that. I didn't know if he was rejecting me because he wasn't attracted to me, or whether it was because he had some misguided sense that I was experimenting with him. But I didn't know how to come up with the conversation without him shutting me down.

On the rugby field we were still electric. We had adapted without Finn, the Golden Trio becoming the Golden Duo. I could see Wesley's appreciation for the rocket that was Rhys Prince growing with every training session, and I knew in my heart that Rhys would be starting every Welsh game in the upcoming Autumn Internationals. If Wesley was sensible, Rhys would be the team's captain within a couple of years.

CHAPTER THIRTEEN - CALLUM

Maybe I was biased. Because Rhys played well and he played beautifully. Seeing him play rugby gave me a real happiness and determination to see this team do well.

In the very first test game against Japan in Cardiff's Millennium Stadium, we thrashed them by over twenty points. That was to be expected though, and New Zealand would be a much harder prospect.

That week, when we flew to Auckland, Rhys sat in the seat next to me on the plane. When turbulence hit and he started to shake more than the plane, his face going grey, I offered him my hand and he threaded his fingers through mine. The other hand clutched the ever-present lion toy. When the turbulence subsided, Rhys moved his hand away but not without a whispered "thanks." I wished I could hold his hand for that little bit longer.

I wondered if there had ever been a couple in the team before. Surely in 200 years of history, there had been gay or bisexual players behind closed doors. If one in every ten men was queer and there were thirty-seven players on the plane...then on average there would be at least another one.

We were roomed together in multiple New Zealand hotels, Wesley wanting to preserve the bonds that had formed between players. Even if I'd wanted a repeat of the previous time, we were so exhausted after every match that we would just get into our beds and fall asleep. We pummelled the club sides that stood against us one by one until we came up against the might New Zealand. It was our turn now to be scared. New Zealand were a team that every team feared. We won the first game against them narrowly, but the second they came back with a ferocity that the Lions simply couldn't match.

Despite his brilliance, Rhys hadn't been selected for either of the matches. It wasn't often that such a new player got put on the squad for the full-on Lions matches, but as far as I was concerned we needed him. The night before the last match I knocked on Wesley's door.

When he answered in just a pair of unicorn-patterned pyjama bottoms I snorted before I could stop myself.

"Not a word," he muttered as he gestured me in to the room.

As soon as the door was shut, I was pleading my case. "Play Prince. Just put him on the field, please."

"Why?" Wesley asked with a wry grin. "Convince me he deserves to be there."

"Well…he plays far better than some of the more experienced players we have on the tour who are starting, he has a much better attitude than some I can name, he's fast, and…he works well with me. I enjoy being captain, but I enjoy it even more when I'm playing with people who understand what I need from them without words."

"Couldn't have put it better myself," said Wesley. "He's playing, I just wanted to check we were working off the same hymn-sheet."

"You were already planning on starting him?" I asked. "That's…great."

"I just hope he doesn't let me down," said Wesley. "Are you ready for your last ever international match?"

"I…think so. Big scary moment."

"Let's get you a win on your last game then. I would like that for you very much."

With Rhys by my side on the pitch, I was confident we could do anything.

14

Chapter Fourteen - Rhys

It was cold on the pitch as we stepped out into the floodlit stadium, the All-Blacks supporters cheer blurred into a roar that penetrated every bone in my body. I had never expected the call-up to play, but Callum's wry smile as we got the news had me realising that perhaps I was not the first to know I'd been chosen. Whether by his intervention or Wesley's hand, I was not just a member of the Lions tour any more. I was a real Lion. And I was ready to play.

The All-Blacks started the game with their haka. Having watched it from the sidelines and on TV before now, it was terrifying to see in person. Just a war dance from fifteen men who stood tiny on the field, but something in the tone and movement made me want to curl up into a ball. The Lions squad stood resolute, lined up on the halfway line with explicit orders from Wesley to show respect to the Maori tradition but to stand and face it head on to show we were not afraid. We would beat them if we stood up to them. And I was determined that we would.

"You ready?" Callum whispered in my ear as we began, so

close that his breath made all the hairs on my neck stand on end.

"I'm ready," I said. I was not going to fuck this chance up.

From the second the whistle blew to start the game, it was carnage. Both teams were determined to win the tour and the game, and the All Blacks got in the first two tries, but neither kick landed as it should so we were ten points down. Before the half-time whistle blew Steve Ford managed to score a try for us that was beautifully converted by our kicker. I hoped Finn was alright at home watching. I'd heard worryingly little from him since we'd been in New Zealand, and I was almost angry that the man who'd gone running to Wesley was taking glory that rightfully could have been his. With both our and New Zealand's defence working overtime we got to half-time with a score of ten-seven to the All Blacks.

"Come on boys, we are capable of more than this," said Wesley in the changing rooms. "We are a team of the best of the best. I have personally selected you to represent our countries in the hope that we get a historic win here in New Zealand. Do not let me down."

Running back onto the pitch five minutes later, his words rang in my head. This could be my last ever test for the Lions as well as my first. I had to prove my own abilities.

As we neared the end of the game we weren't doing any better. A couple of penalties had is at thirteen-ten. One try would have us ahead of New Zealand. One more try against us and they could finish us.

I remembered how Callum had taken advantage of my lack of attack on the field. It was time to test that theory. *Maybe my size is an advantage against these bastards*, I thought. As New Zealand kicked toward our end, I rotated my shoulder. It was

CHAPTER FOURTEEN - RHYS

time to really test months of physio more than I had thus far.

New Zealand kicked short, and their number fifteen caught it with ease. I rushed toward him, but his eyes flicked to the side for a second. Enough for me to realise what he was about to do.

I veered to the blindside as he threw it to his fellow player, and I hit him hard as the ball touched his hands. I was playing dirty, but not illegally. I ripped the ball from him before he could get a good grip on it and left him in the dust. My unexpected move had broken through their offensive line, but their fastest players were already catching up. I ran as far as I could before I felt arms snake around my midriff and I was taken down hard into the dirt. I passed the ball quickly to one of our Irish players, who passed the ball to Callum, whose size let him break the grip of the one player that lunged for him. I scrambled to my feet in time to see him throw himself between the goalposts and over the try-line.

The crowd went wild. It was a majority home crowd for the Kiwis but the try was a fantastic one and one for the history books. With less than two minutes left on the clock we could comfortably draw out our kicking time and take home a win for the series. And I had been part of that.

The team came together on the pitch in a mass of limbs, muddy and gross but with a joy that ran through all of us. We were victorious. Suddenly I could see Callum, and we gave each other a slippery hug.

"You were brilliant," he said. "I'm so, so proud of you."

"You too," I replied, before we were each pulled away into different huddles. Champagne was opened on the pitch and we shook hands with the All Blacks. This was everything I'd dreamed of.

Callum had been named Player of the Match by the TV channels, so I stood just to the side as the interviewer asked him questions about the match. Finally, the interviewer asked the question I knew Callum had been waiting for.

"So, captain of the Lions. What's next for your career?"

"A well earned rest, I think. There'll be no more rugby for me. I've given this game everything I have and to finish here…there's no greater honour." Callum smiled at the stunned interviewer and walked over to join me. I threw an arm around him as we walked toward the player tunnel and into the changing room.

"You've made it official now," I said. "No take-backs."

"I don't want to take it back, these old bones are done."

"*Very* old bones." I walked over to my changing spot and ripped off my sodden and muddy top. I was suddenly aware of how cold I was and ready to get in the hot shower. But I waited for Wesley's grand entrance and speech. He deserved the moment. When he entered the room to cheering and foot stomping and champagne all over his expensive suit, he grinned at us all.

"We fucking did it boys!" he shouted, grabbing a bottle of champagne for himself and having a swig. Apparently, that was the extent of his speech. I pulled off the rest of my clothes and headed for the shower block. Instead of standing at the other end as he usually did, Callum joined me.

"I just cannae believe it," he said, and I just nodded, determined not to look at him too much or think about what had happened between us. "We out to celebrate tonight?"

"I…" I suddenly didn't know. All the other lads were talking about heading to the hotel bar for the celebration of a lifetime, but it all seemed suddenly very overwhelming. And without

CHAPTER FOURTEEN - RHYS

Finn, it almost didn't feel right. "I think I need a minute in the room. To take it all in."

"That I can agree on," said Callum. He seemed to be done washing and stepped out of the shower to grab a towel. I let myself have just the one look as he walked away. His back was toned, and hair only started at his arse, which had a little bit of coverage before his legs took the bulk of the fur. He had bulky thighs and lean calves. He covered himself with a towel and I tore my eyes away, washing myself quickly before heading out to get dressed myself. Callum had dressed in his casual tracksuit and smiled at me. "I'll see you back in the room, yeah?"

I nodded. I took my time getting changed, just soaking up the atmosphere of the win and the chatter around me. I wasn't aware of how empty the changing room had gotten until someone tapped me on the shoulder and coughed lightly. It was Padraig, one of the Irish players, a handsome guy a little bit older than me with dark hair and ice-blue eyes. He leaned in close to my ear so that he could whisper. "I heard you mention you weren't up for celebrating…if you wanted to take the celebration to my room, I'll make sure my room-mate is out."

He passed me a piece of paper and left. Unfolding it, I saw it had a phone number and room number. So I definitely wasn't the only gay in the village. And the thought of getting some of the frustration I'd been feeling about Callum out with a willing volunteer was definitely nice. I packed the last of my kit into the bag and headed for the hotel, just across the road. Wesley hated all the ceremony that came with having a team bus and it was nice to freely walk the road from the stadium to the hotel. I pulled my hood up but waved to any New Zealand fans who did recognise me, and had a couple of pictures with the few British and Irish Lions fans who'd made the trip.

Callum was waiting in the room when I got there, on the phone to his kids from the sound of things. I gave him a smile before heading straight to the bathroom for some…additional preparation. If I was going to be meeting Padraig, I had no idea if he'd want to top, bottom or both. So it was best to be prepared. I texted Padraig to make sure I hadn't completely misread his intentions.

When I went back into the main bedroom Callum was waiting for me. He had poured two glasses of whisky for us, and held one out for me. I joined him where he sat on the bed.

"To us," he said.

"To us," I echoed and knocked it back. Callum poured us each another from a familiar bottle. "Did you bring that from Wales?"

"Aye, I saved it for if we won. Or if we lost. Whisky is the perfect drink for commiserating or celebrating."

My phone buzzed in my pocket, and I checked it quickly.

Padraig: I'm up for whatever you're up for, as long as it's hard ;).

"What's that?" asked Callum.

"Nothing." I quickly flipped my phone away so that he couldn't see the message. It wasn't up to me to out Padraig. And I felt a little ashamed of Callum knowing I'd be hooking up.

"Did I see Padraig's name there?" he asked. "I didn't know you were friends."

"I…we…" I groaned. "He offered to help me celebrate the

CHAPTER FOURTEEN - RHYS

win."

"And by celebrate you mean…" Callum's voice was quiet, but with his low tone even a whisper seemed to carry weight.

"Y'know, do stuff."

"Right." Callum stood up with the bottle of whisky in hand and put it down on the hotel room's desk. He looked somewhere between angry and sad, his eyes and mouth pulled downwards in a grimace. "Better go then, don't want to keep him waiting."

That rankled me. "Fucking hell, I didn't have you down as a prude, Callum."

"I'm not a prude, I…it doesn't matter, does it."

"Are you…judging me?" I asked. "Think I'm making my way round the team or something?"

"Well that's what it looks like to me." Callum's words were like a knife in the chest.

I stood up to face Callum, trying my best to look intimidating even as I had to look up to look him in the eye. "Thanks for that, but if you must know Padraig propositioned me. He's not some straight man who'll get a blowjob from me and then act like it never happened."

"Act like it never happened?" asked Callum. "It's you who fucking…who wanted us to move on. I'd have been with you every night since if you'd just bloody let me."

"What?" I asked, but Callum seemed not to hear as he continued.

He put his hand on the front of my t-shirt and pulled me in, and for a second I thought he was going to start a fight. "And it's you who presumed I was straight."

And suddenly, he was pulling me in close and kissing me. It wasn't tender, not at first as we both worked through the shock of what was happening and fought for some kind of dominance. Teeth clashed and our tongues explored ravenously. I could feel his stubble already starting to rub harshly against my skin. After what could have been seconds or centuries, we both pulled back and looked at one another.

"I am not straight," Callum said. "And I've wanted you since long before this tour. Why don't you want me? Is it something I've done? Or am I just not your type?"

He had let go of my t-shirt, and I stood up on tip-toes for better access to kiss him gently, and slowly. Into the kiss I tried to pour all the want, my emotional and physical feelings for the man. "I want you," I confirmed. "I just didn't want to be some straight guy's messy experiment, or someone you'd look down on for…providing some kind of service."

"Let's…" Callum's eyes drifted over to the bed, and I felt my eyebrows raise involuntarily. "…talk. Can we talk?"

I was hard and straining against my tracksuit bottoms, and could thing of nothing worse than talking. But I nodded and led him by the hand over to the bed, where we laid awkwardly for a second. I glanced down and saw that he was having the same problem as me, cock straining for release against the grey fabric of his joggers.

"So," I said. "Not straight?"

"Nope. Gay. Very gay," Callum said. "Fuck that feels good to say to someone other than Sarah."

I tried not to let the mention of his beautiful wife make me feel less-than, especially given what he'd just said. "How long?" I asked.

"This year I admitted it out loud. Inside though? I think I've had my doubts for a long while. I told Sarah almost a year ago."

"Fuck, I…why haven't you said?"

CHAPTER FOURTEEN - RHYS

"Because I thought you didn't want to know. I thought that… after what had happened, you decided I wasn't your type. That you didn't want me. So I didn't see the point of coming out to you if you were just going to reject me."

"Fucking hell," I said quietly. "I could have been having such great sex for the last month."

Callum chuckled at my lame attempt to make light of the situation. "I'm…sorry, I wasn't more forthright about the situation. I've never been with a man before now, and you'd be right to reject me if you're not looking for a thirty-three year old virgin. But I want you to know that you'd not just be an experiment."

"Then what *are* you looking for?" I asked.

One of Callum's big hands came out to cup my cheek. "If I could promise you the world then I would. But I don't know. I'm going through a divorce, trying to work out how I want to come out and what I want to do with my life now that rugby is over. I have no idea what I'm going to do next. But I do know, right now, that I want you."

I closed the distance between us and kissed him again. We'd had enough talking for my liking. This was a time for actions. Tomorrow morning we could confront whatever new reality we might be facing.

Callum's one hand stayed on my face as we kissed. It felt tender and intimate, and as he stroked down my cheek, my neck, over my t-shirt and to the waistband of my joggers the intimacy of his touch helped to convince me I wasn't some experiment he was going to drop when we were done.

The hand that had drifted to my waistband toyed with it, dipping slightly in at the front like he wasn't sure what to do next. I moved one of my hands down to Callum's joggers and palmed at the hard length straining against the fabric. He moaned into my mouth as my hand worked up a damp spot at the tip of his cock, letting it soak through the thin fabric.

Taking my cue, Callum did the same to me, pushing and grinding with the palm of his hand against the fabric. I pushed up into the touch, unable to stop myself making noises as I did.

"Off," he said between kisses, pushing at the band of my joggers. I used both hands to pull them off and he did the same with his, and I pulled my t-shirt off too. After one long hungry glance, Callum pulled of his top.

We were naked, and staring at one another. For the first time I felt like I had permission to stare. I loved the look of his body, the covering of ginger hair from neck to toe. The slightly old-school rugby player build where he had that little bit more fat than the lads starting out today. I drank it all in with my eyes. "Is this OK with you?" I asked quietly.

"More than OK," he replied. I reached down to clasp my hand around his cock. It was thick enough that my forefinger and thumb just about met and as I gave an experimental stroke a bead of precum leaked from the head. Callum shuddered involuntarily and I swiped over the tip a few times more before bringing my thumb to my mouth and tasting the salty-sweetness of it.

"Do you want…just me to do the touching?" I asked. I knew it was a loaded question, but if he'd not done much of this before then he may want to just let me do the work.

Callum's hand reached out shakily, tentatively to touch my exposed cock and gave it a few tugs that had me arching into him. For a second we just laid and played with each other, and then Callum was kissing me again gently, rolling forward so that he was caging me down to the mattress. I reached down

CHAPTER FOURTEEN - RHYS

to clasp our two cocks together between our bodies. His whole body seemed connected to mine in the moment, from tongues stroking lazily against each other, his hairy chest pressed up against my smooth one all the way down to where his legs locked around mine.

"Does it always feel this good for you?" Callum asked between kisses. "Have I been missing out on this much?"

No, it doesn't always feel this good for me, I wanted to say. *You're special.* "You have been missing out. But I'm sure we can catch up," I said instead.

Callum pushed himself up on his big arms so that his body was leveraged away but his legs still touching mine. "There's something I've wanted to try..."

"Anything," I said. "I'll let you try anything."

And then Callum was off the bed and pulling my legs toward him. He was stood at the end of the bed and my legs were to either side of him. He leaned down to face me again and I felt his thick cock rubbing up against my arse, spreading precum.

"Gonna take some preparation with that thing, bud," I said, only half joking. So much focus on rugby training meant my hookups had been few and far between. And I'd never taken something as intimidating as Callum's cock before.

Callum kissed me gently, but it was over far too quickly. Only the shaking in his arms betrayed any sense of nervousness.

"I want to rim you," he said. "Is that OK?"

"More than OK," I responded, parroting his earlier response. And then his big capable hands were flipping me over so that I was bent over the bed. He leant over me and kissed gently down my back, gently cupping and pulling apart my cheeks before be kissed gently at the exposed, tender skin at my hole. His tongue flicked out gently to taste me and I shuddered, letting out a moan at a pitch I didn't know I had in me. His tongue drew a heavy swipe up from my balls and over the hole again, then gently prodding at my hole as I gripped at the sheets with the feeling. My knuckles were going white where they rested up near my head as Callum's tongue prodded gently at my entrance, sliding in ever so slightly before retreating again. I moaned into the sheets, loving the feeling but desperate for more.

And then he gave me more. One thick finger pushed at my hole gently and I did everything I could to relax enough to let him I. Despite some lubrication, it still wasn't easy but it felt so good to know Callum was filling me. He pushed in and out gently, then crooked his finger upwards and stroked until he found my prostate. I groaned into the bedding as he did. He tried adding a second finger, but I moved away as I felt it try to join.

"Fuck," I groaned involuntarily.

Immediately Callum was up near my face again, the absence of him inside me acute. "Everything OK?" he asked.

"Yes, just...if you're going to do that, I'm gonna need lube," I said.

"Yes. Yes, of course...I don't have lube."

I raised my head from the mattress. "Wallet, bedside table."

I missed the warmth that Callum exuded instantly but I laid and waited til he was back. I felt the cold, slippery touch of his finger again and I groaned as he slid it in. Within seconds a second finger had eagerly joined the first, stroking back and forth inside me and making me want to reach under my body where my cock was trapped against the mattress to stroke myself.

"Fuck, that feels good," I said.

CHAPTER FOURTEEN - RHYS

"Yeah?" asked Callum quietly. He was so self assured, so calm and confident in everything that it was only when he spoke I could hear the nerves at trying all this for the first time. "I really want to..." he started, but let the sentence hang.

"Fuck me?" I asked.

"Yes," he breathed. His fingers didn't stop their relentless intrusion as he leaned back down to cage my body with his and whisper in my ear. "I really, really want to fuck you, Rhys."

"Then fuck me," I said. I needed him in some way now, not just the relentless teasing but his cock in my arse or mouth, just anywhere that I could return the pleasure he was so expertly giving me.

"Do you...have condoms?" he asked.

"PrEP and tested," I replied. "There's one in my wallet if you want to though....oh."

I had tailed off as I felt his fingers swiftly withdraw and then the head of his thick cock was notched against my hole. So we were doing this bare. *Perfect*.

"You sure you want this?" I asked.

"Of course. Are you?" I nodded, and Callum pushed slowly, inch by inch into me.

The stretch and burn was familiar. I winced at the pain but focused on relaxing myself. Callum seemed to have noticed though and stopped pushing. "Everything OK?" he asked.

"All good, good, just...go slow."

Callum hesitated for a second, letting me get used to his massive girth before pushing in slowly, slowly until he was nestled against my back. One big strong arm came to wrap around my chest and he kissed at the side of my neck. I'd never felt so cared for. I had never wanted anyone so much in my life.

As I felt myself adjust, I nodded to Callum and he got the meaning. He pulled out slowly, just a little and we pushed back in. We both moaned in unison. "Fuck, you're so tight. So warm," said Callum. "I should have done this a long time ago."

"Yes, but do it *now*," I whispered back. Callum pulled out slowly again, further the time, and rocked his hips back into me. Other than the movement of his hips and cock, he was plastered to my back, his fur rubbing up against my smooth back as he thrust into me.

As the pace picked up, his momentum driving me down into the mattress, I could feel something building. Where he was so much bigger than I was, his movements getting more and more frantic, my cock was rubbing against the sheets and it felt fucking *good*. My moans rose in volume as his thick cock found my prostate again and again, his breath and sweet kisses along my neck.

"Not…going to…last…" Callum started to warn me, just as I felt my own orgasm building to a crescendo. I came into the sheets beneath me with groan, coating them and my stomach in cum.

Callum pulled out of me, leaving me feeling empty and hollow as he spilled his cum all over my back. He collapsed on his back on the bed beside me and grinned. "Fuck, that felt good," he said.

"Yes…" I said. I felt drunk on the high that had given me. Sex often felt like just a replacement for a hand, not much better than finishing myself off. Sex with Callum felt…different, somehow. Electric. And with how much he cared…

"Come on," he said, sitting up and grabbing my hand. I followed him to the bathroom, where he turned the shower on and pulled me under with him. His hands tenderly touched me

CHAPTER FOURTEEN - RHYS

everywhere as he cleaned me off, occasionally pulling me in for a kiss that my cock responded to with very little energy. He turned off the shower and we dried off together before he led me by the hand back into the bedroom, to his bed — the one not defiled by lube and cum — and pulled me onto his chest. If I'd been any less tired I'd have told him I wasn't a cuddler. But that didn't seem to matter in the moment.

15

Chapter Fifteen - Callum

When I woke up in the morning to a naked muscular form plastered alongside me and blonde hair fanned across one side of my chest, I allowed myself a little smile and huffed to myself.

"Finally awake?" asked Rhys from where he lay.

Feeling a little uncertain of what to do, I reached with one arm to smooth that soft blonde hair down. "I could still be dreaming," I said, well aware of how cheesy I sounded. "Feels like a dream."

"Well real life is my morning breath and sticky-outy hair, so get used to it," said Rhys.

"I can deal with that," I replied. And I could. Because however complicated that sleeping with him might have made things, I had woken up with Rhys Prince in my arms. And that made me feel OK.

He extricated himself from my arms to go to the bathroom, and when he came back he switched on the hotel kettle and started to make himself a tea like he was on automatic. He looked back at me and smiled, adding another mug. I loved how casually he walked around naked. It let me ogle all of him

CHAPTER FIFTEEN - CALLUM

without feeling like a pervert. Well, feeling less like a pervert anyway.

When he climbed back into bed with the mugs and passed me one before curving back into me, resting his hot mug on my chest like I was a table. I didn't mind.

"God, the usual rugby aches and pains are even worse when I've been so worn out by other stuff afterwards," Rhys said, stretching like a cat by my side. I knew how he felt. My calves and biceps always burned from an intense rugby game but the core workout I'd added last night definitely hadn't helped things.

I waited a couple of minutes to see if he'd bring it up again. To give me some sense of how he was feeling.

When he didn't, I spoke. "So...last night," I said.

"Last night," Rhys echoed. "Now."

"What...was it to you?" I asked, afraid it would be just one night. I'd be eternally grateful I even got one night with Rhys Prince. But I wanted more, I was hungry for him now.

Rhys took a long slurp of his tea. "It was great for me," he said. "But I don't know if that was your question."

"No. I..." I struggled for a second to come up with the words. "It was my first time with most of that really, and I don't want you thinking that I'm going to regret it. Because I won't."

"Would you do it again?" Rhys asked.

"In a heartbeat," I said, curving my body toward his so that he could feel my hard morning length press against his leg. He batted it away playfully, and even that sent a thrill of pleasure through me.

"Well I feel the same," he said. "And I'm not one for casual hookups. What happened last night happened because I care for you."

"I care for you too," I said. "I just don't know if I can offer you what you want."

"All I asked was that it happens again," Rhys said.

"I know, I know. I just…life is so fucking complicated. I've got my wife — ex-wife — think about, and my kids. I still haven't come out, and…" I tailed off.

"Well what do you want?" Rhys asked. "Do you want to spread your wings, go try out some guys? I could be like your gay auntie, introducing you to the scene…"

"God no," I said. I hesitated before I carried on, not wanting to sound too creepy. "I only want you. I've only wanted you for a while."

I was worried that might seem a little bit intense, but Rhys just curled his arm around me even tighter. "Good."

"I can't promise much," I said. "But if you want to come and see me in the off season, I'd like that."

"You want me to visit you in Edinburgh?" he asked.

"Of course. I don't know if I'm ready to come out yet, but I want to."

"And until then…" Rhys said, leaving the question hanging in the air.

"Until then, no one will think badly of two professional rugby players and known friends seeing the sights of Edinburgh together for a couple of weeks," I said. "People have seen our chemistry on the pitch, there's no reason for anyone to think that it translates to the bedroom."

Rhys took a long slurp of his tea. We both jumped when his phone vibrated, like it had interrupted some serene peace.

"Fuck," he laughed. "Padraig is not thrilled I left him hanging last night."

I let out an involuntary growl. "Is he now?"

CHAPTER FIFTEEN - CALLUM

"Not jealous, are you?" Rhys asked.

"Aye," I admitted. "If I wasn't so jealous last night we wouldn't have done anything, so I'm not going to apologise for it."

"Well I guess I'll let him down gently then," Rhys teased.

"I know I have no right to ask...but can we keep this between us?" I asked.

"Don't worry, your secret's safe with me," Rhys said.

"I mean, can we keep doing this between us. I won't be hooking up with anyone else and I'm hoping you'll do the same."

"I'd like that," said Rhys. "So what are we? I know I won't be telling anyone, I just want to know where we stand in my head."

"Well...if you can handle me being closeted, I don't know if it's a bit early to get the word *boyfriend* involved-"

"No, boyfriend is fine with me," said Rhys.

"Boyfriend it is then," I replied. I pulled him in closer to me, and looked over at the bed we'd left the night before. "I bloody hope the cleaning staff are discreet about it."

***

Home was...weird. Having left Rhys at the gates of Auckland airport so he could take the plane back to Bristol and drive to Cardiff, whereas I was flying straight to Edinburgh, it felt like we were leaving things in limbo before we even got started. Like a school-yard romance where two kids called each other boyfriend and girlfriend for a couple of weeks and then never talked again. It had been a week, but our victory parade through the streets of Edinburgh wasn't far away.

But I had to remember after the highs of a winning rugby

tour and captaining my team to victory, that I had real life responsibilities too. Responsibilities that I loved, but responsibilities all the same.

"Why are those people staring at you, Daddy?" asked Logan as I held his hand, walking him through the aquarium in Fife. At ten years old he was too old to be holding my hand really, but he hadn't let go and I didn't mind.

"Because I'm very handsome and famous," I replied. Sarah laughed at my side.

"Sharks!" he shouted, letting go of my hand and leading his older sister over to the pretty pathetic looking sharks as she rolled her eyes but followed anyway.

"Thanks for doing this," I said to her. "It can't be easy, all the..stares and stuff."

"I'm used to it," she said. "Years of being married to the best rugby player in Scotland."

"And now we're not married, and I'm not the best rugby player in Scotland," I said.

Sarah held up her empty hand, where the tan lines and gentle warping of the skin betrayed there had recently been a wedding ring. It was weird, seeing it gone. But mine had been gone since we made the announcement.

"The six weeks of you going away helped me," she said. "Every time you've gone before I've been waiting at home for you. But this time…I think this time let me be single."

"Are you saying you…" I asked.

"No, God no. I'm not ready for any of that yet. We've been married twelve years, I'm not about to jump into bed with someone else."

I felt something roiling in my gut, like I was about to be sick all over the lovely sting-ray petting pool that the kids had now

CHAPTER FIFTEEN - CALLUM

run over to. "Fair enough," I said, hoping she wouldn't notice anything different in my expression.

It was nice for us to have had a day out as a family, I thought, as I drove us back the hour from Fife to Edinburgh. The kids would be staying with their mother for the week, and I...I had a guest staying with me.

"You going to be OK all by yourself this week?" asked Sarah.

"I've got one of the rugby lads staying over," I said, half-honestly.

Sarah saw right through my attempt at deception. "Rhys Prince?"

"...yes." I was conscious that the kids were in the back of the car, and so was Sarah. She blew out a breath, obviously trying to decide what to say.

"Just...be safe, and think of us," she said.

"I will. I promise," I replied. I reached over to give her a hug, but she was out of the car before I could. I waved goodbye to the kids as they trooped into our old family home, and I let myself just have a minute to miss it. To miss laying in bed next to my wife.

Before I could look to the future.

***

I looked around the little living space and open plan kitchen, wanting to make sure everything was clean. I was never normally much of a clean freak — having two kids had successfully knocked much pride out of me when it came to cleanliness. But I didn't want Rhys to think *I* lived like a slob.

I plumped up the cushions on the sofa again, and sprayed a bit of Febreze around the place. I was spiralling, going into panic mode. So I did exactly what Rhys would do, and boiled the kettle for two cups of tea.

A knock came to the door and I wiped my palms on my jeans before opening it. And there he was. Rhys' hair had been pushed back and he was wearing a hoodie and jeans, trailing a suitcase behind him;.

"Hey you," he said. He stepped into the flat and closed the door. And for a second neither of us moved. And then we both did at once, and my hands were tangled in his hair and his in mine as I was leaning to kiss him.

Our lips met and for the first time since we met there was complete joy in them. There was very little guilt, there was freedom, and for once it seemed like we were both on the same page. I yanked at the bottom of his hoodie and the t-shirt below and for just a second we were forced to separate so that I could get it over his head.

Every time I saw that body I wanted to touch every part of it. And now, in the privacy of my little apartment, I could.

"Are you done looking?" he asked with a cheeky grin, "because I'm happy for you to just keep touching."

"Touching, huh?" I asked. I put one hand on his now bare chest and pushed him back towards the door. He hissed as his back touched the cold wooden surface. "How's this for touching?"

I leaned down to kiss him again, keeping him pushed up against the door as I fumbled clumsily with both hands on his belt. Once that was done I pulled his trousers down just enough to pull out his hardening cock. I moved away from kissing at his mouth to kiss his neck as I played with his erection.

"That's…good," he said now that his mouth was free. I smirked against his neck and lowered myself to kiss at his

CHAPTER FIFTEEN - CALLUM

chest, flicked a tongue over his nipples, then let my mouth keep travelling downward over perfect washboard abs. I was about to do something I never had before, but surely I knew what I was doing, right?

I sank to my knees on the cold tile of my hallway, bringing myself eye level with Rhys' cock. I swiped my tongue tentatively over the leaking head and Rhys' low groan encouraged me to swipe at it once again. The pre-cum was salty-sweet and not at all what I had expected. For a few moments, I licked and teased at the head, too nervous to go much further.

With my hand in place as a buffer I let myself take his cock slightly deeper into my mouth. One of Rhys' hands tangled in my hair, gently encouraging me to take him in. Despite my nerves, my own cock was like steel in my trousers and I loosed my grip on him so that I could pull mine out. I sank his cock into my mouth until I gagged, pulling back only for Rhys to gently encourage me back again. Every time I got too far and gagged, I felt my cock jump in my hand. I wasn't sure if I liked the sensation of gagging on a cock but something subconscious and primal was spurring me on.

"Just like that," Rhys said as I gagged once more. Keeping my right hand on my cock, I let my left explore, playing with his heavy balls for a minute before travelling backward to toy with the cleft of his arse. Rhys had started to gently thrust into my mouth, the hand holding my head on place so I stroked my cock to the rhythm he was setting.

"Your mouth...feels so good," he said. I could taste the saltiness of his pre-cum as he continued to push into my mouth, and the thought of making him feel so good made me feel so good.

I pulled off to run my tongue down his thigh and back up

again before looking up at him. "I want to make you cum," I said.

Rhys grinned down at me and guided my mouth back to his cock. His thrusts got more urgent and I stroked my cock to match them. Every time he hit the back of my throat I'd gag, and he'd moan, and that made my sweet release edge ever fucking closer.

"I think I'm gonna cum," said Rhys. "Do you want it on you?"

I shook my head gently and kept my mouth on him. If he was going to finish, I wanted to taste it. Rhys rocked his hips into my mouth a couple more times before finishing. I did my best to swallow the bitter saltiness that was coating the inside of my mouth but gagged as I pulled off, it running down my chin as I frantically stroked myself to finish all over my floor.

Rhys looked down at me with that same grin on his face. His cheeks were flushed and his hair sticking up at the back from where he'd writhed against the door. "Damn," he said, offering a hand to pull me up. "Never had you down as submissive."

I took his hand with one of mine and wiped at my chin as I stood. It was weird how normal this was. How easy it could be. How much I enjoyed taking on a completely different role every time Rhys and I had sex.

"I…" I didn't know what to say. "I'll just clean all this up."

Rhys followed me into the living area with his suitcase, tucking himself back into his jeans discretely as he did so. "How's retired life?" he asked.

I ran out to the hallway with a kitchen towel to mop up the mess I'd made before answering. "It's weird, I guess. But it's only been a week so I'm not expecting a world of change yet. It's been nice to spend time with the kids."

"When are they next back round?" he asked.

CHAPTER FIFTEEN - CALLUM

"Next Monday, once I've kicked your sorry arse out. They don't want to see their dad shagging on every surface in the flat," I grinned.

"So pinning me up against the door was just the start of a war against the bedroom, was it?" Rhys shot back.

"Shut up," I said. "Oh, there's a tea for you there. It might be cold. We were otherwise occupied."

"Thanks," said Rhys. I dragged his suitcase into the bedroom and joined him on the sofa, sipping tea out of a mug that said *World's Best Rugby Player*, with a picture of one of my teammates on it. Sarah had thought it was hilarious, once upon a time, and it had come with me to the house.

"Looking forward to the parade?" I asked.

"Like a hole in the head," he replied. "I just want to get back to rugby. I know some people love the glory but I don't. All the attention gets me off my game."

"You're the prettiest rugby player I know," I said. I let my spare hand rest on his and he didn't move away. "You're always going to get more attention, especially with how well you play. Talking of attention, how's Finn doing?"

Rhys grimaced. "About as well as you'd expect. He doesn't think he'll be selected to play for the Wales squad in the next Autumn series. At least he still has Cardiff Old Navy to fall back on for now."

"For now?" I asked. Rhys' fingers twisted around my own, and I could see the concern in his eyes.

"He's being stupid, drinking enough in the evening that it's obvious in training the next day. Finn's off his game and he won't be starting games if he keeps this kind of behaviour up."

"Well shit," is all I could think to say. I'd spent my whole career up til this point maintaining my image alongside the game. I was *proud* of the fact that being the *Gentleman of Rugby* meant that people thought I was a good role model for their kids, and that the profile had led to broadcasters clamouring for my punditry now I was a free agent. I couldn't imagine giving it all up in the way Finn had.

And I was determined that I never would.

16

Chapter Sixteen - Rhys

I was determined to let Callum take all the limelight in the victory parade. He was our captain, after all, and we were in his hometown. I didn't want to take that attention from him. I wanted him to bask in the success of winning a rugby tour just one more time.

But the media, and Callum, didn't seem to want that. He'd pulled me forward at any opportunity to wave at the front of the bus with him. "You deserve this," he said. "You had the best debut of anyone I've ever seen. I want you to see the papers in a decade and know how far you've come."

When I woke up with him the morning after the victory parade, he smiled down at me and mussed my hair. "You've made an impression," he said.

He was right. Every sports website and rugby fan forum was filled with pictures of the two of us smiling and waving down at the crowd. One headline stood up. *The Retiring Gentleman of Rugby and its new Crown Prince.*

I laughed, but Callum turned my head to face him. He was laying on the pillow with his red hair sticking everywhere but his face was deadly serious. "You take this an you run with it," he said. "I want people in ten years to forget I ever existed, you'll be so good. I want you captaining the team that wins all three matches out in New Zealand."

I felt my cheeks heat up and he kissed me. "Right, tea."

We whiled away almost the whole week in the flat with the odd foray out into Edinburgh. Every time we left the flat to do something a sneaky photo of the two of us out and about would end up in the media. We went to restaurants a couple of times, even out to Edinburgh castle to see the sights. But due to the ever-present media and people with smartphones we kept a friendly distance.

I'd played around with closeted guys before, but I'd never dated one. And the reality was a mix and match of emotions. I loved every second I spent with him, even keeping our distance and acting friendly as we toured Edinburgh. And then our days and nights in his little flat were electric, spent with constant body contact and our lips exploring the others' body. Every morning that I woke up in a tangle of limbs with Callum felt like the new best morning of my life.

On Sunday morning, our last, Callum took me on a walk through Edinburgh to Holyrood Park. It was nothing like the flat expanses of parkland I knew from Cardiff and London. Arthur's Seat was a dormant volcano that rose high above the Edinburgh landscape and Callum insisted on climbing it so that we could see the whole of the city from where we sat near its peak. It was quiet, and people seemed to be enjoying the view rather than looking at us, so he snuck me his hand. The sun was high in the sky, and things felt blissful for a moment.

"I wish it could always be like this," he said. "Just you and me. Holding hands like nobody's watching."

CHAPTER SIXTEEN - RHYS

"And why can't it be?" I ventured. "More like...when do you think it can be?"

"I..." Callum started, but then he was snatching his hand away from mine and standing up, dusting off his jeans. "Hi, I didn't expect to see you here!"

"Obviously..." drawled one of the ladies walking toward us. As I took notice of them I realised that one of them was Callum's ex-wife, Sarah.

Trooping up behind them were both kids I'd seen on FaceTime and framed in pictures around Callum's flat. My heart stuttered in my chest with nerves. How was I meant to act? How should I approach the whole situation? Did Sarah know about me? Did the older lady? Sarah's face was a blank canvas, but the way the older woman's eyes narrowed at the night of me told me she had me figured out. And she didn't like what she was seeing.

"Daddy!" shouted the youngest kid, Logan, as he launched himself toward Callum. Olivia just gave him a smile and a quick hug.

"How are you both, huh?" he asked. As they chattered away to him I realised he had gone into complete Dad mode. And I was left facing his wife and the other woman alone.

"Hi, I'm Rhys. Nice to meet you," I said. Sarah smiled politely but the older woman looked me up and down before speaking.

"Yes, we know who you are," she said.

Ah. I wanted to believe it was from all the newspaper coverage but her expression wasn't exactly screaming *big rugby fan meeting breakout star of the tournament.* It was more *school matron meets truant.* I noticed she also hadn't given me her name.

Finally after what felt like an age of silence Callum came

over to talk to us. "Rhys, you've met Sarah, my...ex-wife, and Elizabeth. My ex-mother-in-law."

Ah. So that was why Elizabeth looked at me with murder in her eyes. If Sarah knew all about Callum's sexuality, it made sense that she would have spoken to her mother. And it made sense that her mother would see an openly gay friend of Callum's as a threat. She was right, but it didn't mean I liked the assumption.

"What brings you both up here? Casual walk amongst *friends?*" Elizabeth asked.

"Yes, that's it Elizabeth." I could see Callum's jaw tighten as he spoke. It was like everything in him tensed up around her, and I could see why. Both Callum and Sarah looked at one another, then back at the kids to make sure they were out of earshot.

Then Sarah spoke. "Now isn't the time for this, Mum. Callum, I'll drop the kids off to you tomorrow morning, alright?"

Callum nodded and turned to say goodbye to the kids. Sarah and Elizabeth both continued to appraise me. I hadn't felt so much like I was at a cattle auction since the very first day of academy rugby. As they both turned to go, Elizabeth hit Callum with a pointed glare. "Do think of the children now, won't you?"

"I always do, Elizabeth. You know that." Callum said. We watched as they trooped down the path away from us until they were out of sight. When I looked at Callum, the set of his jaw was tense.

"She really gets to you, doesn't she?" I asked.

"No," Callum muttered, but I could see in the way he held himself that he'd completely closed off.

CHAPTER SIXTEEN - RHYS

"Let's go," I said, reaching out to tug his arm. I had very little time before my train and didn't want to spend it with Callum sulking about something we couldn't control.

We were almost to the bottom of the hill when Callum finally spoke up. "You know, even if I wasn't gay I wonder if Elizabeth might have pushed me and Sarah apart sooner or later," he said.

"Really? How come?"

"Well, you saw her just now. She wasn't just talking like that because I'm Sarah's ex. She's talked like that since the day we met. For a while, I thought it was because I wasn't good enough for Sarah. It's not like an academy rugby player is on fantastic wages, and it definitely wasn't the case fifteen years ago. I worked my way up through the squad, started getting sponsorship deals and earning enough money to get Sarah whatever she wanted...then I realised that nothing I could have done would make her happy that Sarah was with me, or anyone. Elizabeth thrives on being needed by people. And me being around meant Sarah needed her a little bit less."

"So why do you care now?" I asked. "Not trying to be too nosey, but...she's out of your life now, at least as much as she can be."

"Because she's old fashioned and very traditional," Callum said. "Sarah's told her why we split and she doesn't like it. And I don't want her poisoning Logan's mind. He's so young, so happy. The thought of her stamping on that joy for life and the happiness he gets just from being himself is enough to make her want to keep me on side."

"So how the hell do you move forward with your life?" I asked. I looked around to check we were far enough away from other people before talking again. "How do you take away that influence and move forward, come out, be yourself?"

"I don't know, " Callum admitted. He looked completely defeated. Not caring who was round, I yanked him into a rough hug.

Later, on the train home I worried about our relationship for the very first time. I knew Callum wasn't out. I knew that I'd have to make sacrifices and that his family would always come first. My biggest worry now was that he might never come out, and that I might be stuck in this little limbo between him and Elizabeth forever.

17

Chapter Seventeen - Callum

I couldn't bring myself to hold a candle for Cardiff in quite the same way I did Edinburgh. The city was nice enough, sure, but it didn't have Edinburgh's picturesque peaks and the castle wasn't on top of a sleeping volcano, so that lost it some cool points.

I stepped off the train at Cardiff's Central Station and made my way down Westgate Street toward the two stadia that dominated the centre of the city - the Millennium Stadium in all its glory and the smaller Arms Park as an extension at its side.

As far as Rhys was concerned, I wasn't due down for another couple of days. Sarah had insisted on taking the kids early this weekend so that they could go and watch a new film she'd been dying to see, and I had used the chance to sneak out of Scotland and to the little capital city in Wales. It had taken almost ten hours on the train and I was aching, but the walk helped to clear my head. Unemployed life had been great so far with the kids to entertain me but I knew without them I needed to find something to do.

So I'd decided on surprising my boyfriend, and getting the added pleasure of getting to watch him play his Saturday evening game. It had been three weeks since he'd left Edinburgh and I was aching to see him in the flesh. Being closeted and being in a long distance relationship were two things that were playing hell with my emotions.

"One terrace ticket, please," I said at the ticket office. I noticed the exact second in which the lady recognised me by the sudden widening of her eyes. She passed me the ticket with a vacant smile.

I stopped by the club shop to buy myself a scarf. I considered buying myself one for the South African side that they were playing but decided that would get me in too much trouble with him, so I stuck with actually supporting his team. I grabbed myself a pint from the bar and headed out to take my place in the stands.

The Arms Park was old-fashioned in a way that some saw as becoming outdated but that I saw as old-school cool in a way that most stadiums couldn't hope to be. They'd retained their terraced stands in some places rather than seats and I leaned on the metal bar as the stadium steadily filled up around me. It was early October, and things were already getting a little colder in the evenings. I was glad I had a pint of lager to warm my belly.

A couple of people noticed me and asked for photos, and I was as nice as possible in letting them get some good snaps. I was recognised much less here than I was in Edinburgh - people supported their country's stars more than anything else and once everyone's attention turned to the game I could blend in with the rest of the crowd.

When the team ran out I was shocked to see Finn amongst

CHAPTER SEVENTEEN - CALLUM

them. He looked a little bit drawn even from afar and I could see he wasn't as alert as usual. Losing the Lions spot had really done a number on him.

When Rhys ran out, the crowd went wild. He was their new Welsh prince and he was by far the squad's biggest draw. He'd come so far from a guy who was so excited to get on the pitch for Wales just seven months ago. I realised it had been almost a year since a major injury had almost taken him out. I wouldn't guess it now from his performance. He dodged and weaved other players when he had the ball, barely allowing anyone to get a tackle in on him. And when the opposition had the ball his speed let him get hit after hit in on any player. He was made for rugby.

When the game ended with a storming victory for Cardiff, I was one of the first on the pitch to greet the players and shake their hands. Some greeted me like an old friend and some with suspicion or hostility — since my retirement I'd been linked with coaching some Scottish teams in the Premiership, and it must have looked to some of the players here like I was spying or ready to poach them.

It was a few minutes before the crowd of fans around Rhys thinned enough that I could see him and he could see me. As soon as he caught my eye his face split into a grin, and he waved off the fans as politely as he could before walking up to me. There was a moment of awkwardness as he assessed what we could do in public, but I reached out my arms and pulled him into a smelly hug. He smelled of sweat and mud and grass, and his hair was soaked from perspiration and rolling around on the ground. But he was my Rhys, in my arms. Very few things made me happier.

"What are you doing here?" he asked, pulling away from the

hug to take some more selfies with fans who didn't even seem to register I existed. "I thought you weren't coming down for days!"

"Kids are with Sarah," I said. "And I wanted to watch you play." I watched as a blush ran up Rhys' tanned skin and he cleared his throat. "I'll meet you at the flat?"

Rhys nodded and I headed out to the main road, treading slowly to reach the front door to Rhys' block of flats. A couple of fans in scarves and hats nodded and smiled to me as they passed, and a couple of people honked loud vuvuzelas. I knew Rhys would be a little while so I stood under the eaves of the front door and warmed my hands by rubbing them together. When he finally rounded the corner in a hoodie it took everything I had not to throw myself at him.

"C'mon," he muttered, his hand briefly brushing mine as he walked past me. "I've missed you and…"

He didn't need to finish the sentence because I felt it too. That shiver of energy than ran between us whenever we touched that I missed since leaving the rugby field. Rhys gave me energy like seventy-thousand roaring fans in the stand. And he was all mine.

I followed him up the stairs. The corridor was dark and no one was around. Before he could get the key in the lock I was at his back, nipping at the smooth exposed skin of his neck and leaving tiny marks as I explored the front of his body with my hands.

Rhys leaned back into me even as his hand shook with trying to get the key in the lock. "What if someone sees?" he asked.

"Then let them see," I said. But I held back to let him get the key in the lock. I didn't really want this to be my public outing.

As soon as the door was open we practically fell through

CHAPTER SEVENTEEN - CALLUM

it and Rhys' mouth was on mine in seconds. I slammed the door shut with my heel and started clawing at the bottom of his hoodie to bring it over his head. I wanted my hands on his body and I wanted that yesterday.

He hissed as my freezing cold hands found the skin at the small of his back. I pushed him through the bedroom door and onto the bed, finally pulling off his t-shirt so that he was blissfully naked from the waist up in front of me.

I yanked at his jeans to bring them down and his boxers came with them even as he shucked off his shoes. There were clothes littering the floor and I hadn't even started undressing yet. I kissed down his body to his leaking cock, giving an quick lick before I lowered myself to bring his jeans over his ankles so that he was completely naked.

I stood back to appraise his naked body, urgency gone now I had what I wanted in front of me. I unbuttoned my coat slowly and let it and the scarf drop to the floor. Rhys' eyes followed it and I let my jumper and t-shirt follow suit. All that was left to do was remove the lower half of my garments.

I wanted to extend the tension of the situation, so I turned away from him as I took off my shoes and socks and lowered my jeans and pants. I yelped in the most unmanly way as I felt a sharp pain on my arse cheek, then turned to face Rhys. "Did you just bite me?" I asked.

"You were taking a long time and your arse looks good. Makes me want to reconsider bottoming tonight."

I tackled him to the bed. "Your arse is mine tonight, boy. Any other time I'd be up for it." I said it with more confidence than I felt. Other than the odd experimental finger I hadn't ever done much in the way of preparing myself for a future of bottoming. I'd presumed from porn dynamics that I'd always end up topping. But the thought of bottoming for Rhys was... interesting.

I kissed him again before moving down to his smooth neck, and then to his chest. Rugby had left him with bruises and I made sure to kiss each one in turn as I worked my way down his body until I was kneeling on the floor in front of him. I teased at the head of his cock with my tongue before kissing down the side of his stomach, my cheek rubbing against his cock as my mouth moved closer to his legs. I might have been pretty new to the world of gay sex, but something about being with Rhys just made it feel instinctual, primal. I knew how to make myself feel good and by extension it wasn't so difficult to figure out what made Rhys tick.

"You fucking tease," Rhys whispered. I licked a strip back up his stomach just to piss him off before kissing back downwards again, nuzzling between his thigh and his balls before taking one of them into my mouth. He moaned, low and deep, a noise that made my cock twitch.

"Come up here, I want to try something," said Rhys before I could push up his legs to tease his hole with my tongue. I slid back up his body thinking he wanted me above him but he gestured for me to lay down on my back. I laid on the bed and Rhys manoeuvred himself so that he was straddling my face. I couldn't see his face through his legs but I felt as the warmth of his mouth engulfed my cock.

Rhys' arse inched closer to my face and I knew what he wanted. I parted his cheeks with my thumbs and ran my tongue from the back of his balls, over his taint and to his tight hole. When he groaned on my cock, the vibrations sent shivers through me. I licked and prodded at his hole with my tongue as he sucked on my cock, and every moan and groan

CHAPTER SEVENTEEN - CALLUM

I managed to prise out of him just added directly to my own pleasure. After a few blissful minutes, Rhys moved himself so that he was facing me.

"Why'd you move?" I asked, but Rhys said very little as he reached over to the bedside table to pull out the little tube of lube. I had to resist licking my lips as he reached back to prepare his hole, then slicked up my cock with the lube. "Do you want to fuck me?" he asked.

"Y-yes," I replied. Rhys straddled me and positioned my cock carefully at the edge of his hole.

"Or would you rather I fuck myself on you?" he asked, then he impaled himself on my cock in one quick motion. I yelped in pleasure as I was suddenly engulfed in the hot, tight heat of him.

Rhys pulled up and then thrust himself down again, and every movement made us groan in harmony. He built up a steady rhythm but the strain of doing so had him covered in a sheen of sweat in minutes. He rested on one hand and used the other to stroke himself as I watched. "Damn, you're beautiful," I said. He grinned and panted through open lips as he continued to spear himself on my cock.

He kept up a pace that drove me insane. It was quick enough to give me so much pleasure but not enough to edge me to the point of orgasm that I was craving. But I let Rhys keep up the pace. Longer sex was not a complaint in my eyes.

Rhys started to shudder on top of me and the pace stuttered as he groaned. "Fuck, Callum. I'm going to..."

"Finish all over me, baby," I said. Rhys stroked himself hard and fast and came over me and the bed with a groan. He fell forward onto me, his hands on either side of my head.

"Fuck me," he said quietly. I let my hands lock around the

back of his neck and I pulled him toward me to kiss, finally allowing myself to set the pace. I jackhammered into him as fast as I could. He laid almost flat on me, cum and sweat immaterial as I got closer to the point of finishing. I groaned as I got close, so close…and then I was finishing inside him, locked together to the hilt and covered in bodily fluids.

Rhys laughed as he leaned back, easing me out of him gently. "Gross," he said, looking down at the mess he had made all over my stomach and chest. I swiped one hand down his sticky chest and we both laughed. Sex *was* gross, but it was great when it was with Rhys.

He walked over to the bathroom door. "Two minutes?" he asked, and I nodded. I heard the shower turn on and waited patiently for the allotted time. I knew I'd join him in the shower and we would kiss languidly, sensually and wash the sex off one another. I knew afterwards we would cuddle and either watch a film or sleep. I knew him, and loving him was instinctual. I just wished I had the courage to move our relationship into the outside world.

***

I stroked idly at Rhys's hair as he laid on my chest. We seemed to sleep apart when we first got into bed, but found each other in the night. Every single night.

For once, I seemed to be the one who was awake first. Rhys had always been an early riser, but the rugby game and last night's fun seemed to have taken it out of him. I enjoyed listening to his heavy breaths and the feeling of his hard, toned body pressed up against my softer one. The advantage of having more body fat meant I was an excellent pillow.

CHAPTER SEVENTEEN - CALLUM

"Huh? Who stole the yellow weasel?" Rhys looked up at me with his eyes blank and unknowing before they came into focus. "Sorry. Weird dream."

His phone buzzed, and I kissed him gently even as I held in a laugh. "Must have been a very strange dream."

"The strangest dream is falling in lo…for a retired Scottish rugby player," he said.

"Hey, I wasn't retired when you started falling for me," I joked. "Though now I know it was a dream of yours…maybe I should get to pinch you wherever I like to make sure you're not dreaming."

His phone buzzed again, but Rhys' hand drifted between my thigh and my chest as he laughed. "Either way, a retired rugby player is very much what I got."

The phone buzzed again. "You're popular this morning," I said.

"Ignore it. I bet it's my mum finally watching the match on catch-up," he said.

"Ignore it? what would you have me do instead?" I asked. Rhys started toying with my morning wood idly as we kissed slowly. There was no urgency in the morning and I loved it.

His phone started buzzing relentlessly then as he got a call. "For fuck's sake!" he rolled over to grab his phone. "I'll just silence this and then…oh fuck. Oh fuck, fuck, fuck."

My heart beat an irregular rhythm at his words. Had we been found out? Had someone died? "What's up?" I asked.

"I don't even know if I want you to…ah, fuck it. Just see for yourself."

Rhys passed his phone to me with his eyes covered dramatically. I wasn't prepared for what I saw on screen. Finn Roberts, obviously having had a drink from the way his eyes weren't in focus, looking up at the camera with a penis in his mouth. From what I could see it looked like the video had been taken outdoors as he was kneeling on grass. He was an enthusiastic participant to say the least.

"Did he send this to you?" I asked. I had no idea how much Rhys had told him about our relationship but I still didn't want him sending this kind of thing out of the blue. Rhys was *mine.*

"No, no. It's all over Twitter. The whole team has been texting me asking if I've seen him, if he's OK, and there are journalists reaching out to me for comment like it's something I should care about."

"Call him," I said. "Call him now."

I waited as Rhys dialled and called Finn's number but no answer came. My heart felt like it had migrated up my throat and into my mouth as I thought of what Finn was going through. And how he'd been so stupid as to let this get out. "Does he live nearby?" I asked.

Rhys nodded. "We'll walk, see if he's home. I worry that where the video was taken...he might not have made it home."

Oh shit. Of course. Rhys' concern had been instantly with his safety, mine with his sexuality. My priorities were all fucked up.

We both dressed quickly and Rhys led me down Westgate Street and back toward the station. Instead of getting on a train we took a few side-streets that led us to a long promenade. At the end, I could just about make out the blue glint of water. "He lives in a flat above Cardiff Bay," Rhys said in explanation.

We walked past some high-rises, much more modern than Rhys' place from the outside. When we got to the right one, Rhys tapped out a code at the front door and then pulled out a key as we ascended the stairs.

CHAPTER SEVENTEEN - CALLUM

"You have a key to his place?" I asked. It was stupid that I was getting jealous over something like that, but I wondered why.

"I have several in a drawer at home. You wouldn't believe how often he loses his keys and I have to get him a new one, so I made him get a whole load cut." Rhys smiled as he opened the front door. "Now prepare yourself."

He opened the door, stepping inside and beckoning me in before closing it again behind the both of us. The smell of alcohol and sweat was immediately an assault on my nose and the place didn't look much better. It was a studio flat with just a door off the main room that I presumed led to a bathroom, but the rest was all packed into one small living space. Finn was snoring, as naked as the day he was born splayed on top of the mattress, a spilt beer bottle soaking into the bedding. There were cans of energy drinks and beer bottles littering the floor and the whole place was disgustingly untidy.

"Oh, mate," said Rhys gently. I squeezed his hand in reassurance before he stepped forward to open the curtains to let light into the room.

"Fuck off," groaned Finn. Rhys opened all the windows along one wall to get fresh air into the room and then went into the kitchen to grab a recycling bag, picking up cans and bottles as he did. I realised this wasn't the first time he'd done all this. It was all so routine. Finn really was in a bad place.

"Get some fucking clothes on," said Rhys. "I've tried to help you but it's time for some fucking tough love."

"What the fuck have I done this time?" asked Finn. "It's not a crime to get drunk after a game is it? Just because you're a boring twat doesn't mean the rest of us have to be."

"Lose the tone, get some clothes on and we can talk. Or I'll set the Scotsman on you."

Rhys looked pointedly at me and Finn followed his gaze. He flinched as soon as he laid eyes on me. I did my best to put the same stern tone on that I adopted when Olivia and Logan refused to share the XBOX. "I suggest you do as Rhys says."

Suddenly aware of his own nudity, Finn grabbed at the sheets to cover himself and grabbed a pair of pyjama shorts from the floor. Rhys put the full recycling bag to one side of the room and started boiling the kettle in Finn's tiny kitchen. Tea was his answer to all of life's biggest problems.

"I. Thought. You. Were. Dead." He punctuated each syllable with a sugar in one of the cups. I gently nudged him out of the way and distributed the sugar evenly between the cups to avoid any of us having a heart attack. I laid one hand on the small of his back and rubbed it gently in the hope of calming him down. He seemed to deflate and sank into my side. Finn's eyes followed every movement. I handed him two mugs and he took one over to Finn. Rhys pulled his phone out of his pocket and handed it to Finn. I watched as the colour drained from Finn's face.

"What the fuck?" he said. "Where'd you get this?"

"Twitter," Rhys said. "It's all over the place at the moment. Twitter, Reddit, some news sites are going to pick this up."

"But…that was weeks ago! That wasn't last night!" Finn half shouted.

"Don't think it matters when it happened mate, it matters that it did. And I don't know how you're going to get yourself out of this one."

I felt like I was intruding on a very private moment, like I wasn't meant to be there. But neither of them asked me to leave. Finn rested his head on Rhys' shoulder and groaned.

CHAPTER SEVENTEEN - CALLUM

"What are they going to do, fire me for sucking cock?"

Rhys pushed him. "I'm gay, that is not the problem hare. The problem is you having sex in a public place with someone willing to post it all over the fucking internet. The *problem* is that at some point, something you do is going to be the straw that breaks the camel's back and fucks up your career, or worse."

None of us said anything for a minute. I took a too-loud slurp of tea and Finn looked up like he'd forgotten he was there. "What's Callum Anderson doing in my kitchen?"

"Moral support as I save your sorry arse," Rhys said.

"So he's been…staying with you, has he?" Finn asked. Rhys looked hopelessly at me for a second like he wasn't sure what to say.

"Rhys and I are together, if that's what you're implying. Unlike you, we're not having too much trouble keeping it quiet now."

Rhys glared at me for my harshness but Finn gave a humourless laugh. "Fair play, mate. Fair play."

"Right, get your phone plugged in," said Rhys to Finn. "We're going to tackle the problem, and tackle it head on. You're going to need to tell me if there are other videos like this, I'll call the coach to get ahead of the news and keep your place on the squad, and-"

Finn put a hand on Rhys' chest. "No offence, mate, but I think I'm done."

"Done?" asked Rhys.

"Yeah. I've fucked up so many times, and rugby…it just isn't helping. I'm on a downward spiral and I…" I noticed a tear leak from Finn's eye, and he turned away from Rhys to wipe it away. "I need to go and find help. I need to be away from…all this."

"...right." Rhys pulled Finn in for a tight hug. "How can I help you to do that?"

I was a spare part for the next couple of hours as he and Finn worked over Finn's plans. I made about twenty million cups of tea and ordered in some takeaway food as they discussed what came next. When we finally left and the light was fading outside, Rhys put one arm around me and hugged me halfheartedly.

"I remember when we were a Golden Trio," he said. "Just me left now."

"I'm sticking around," I said. "I'm not going to let you down."

But something inside me stirred, those stupid little feelings that had sprung up the night before. What if I wasn't ready enough for Rhys? What if I couldn't do the right thing like Finn, and face up to my fear?

As I looked into Rhys' deep green eyes, I knew I had to do the right thing for him eventually. Whether that be standing proudly beside him, out and proud, or letting him go.

18

Chapter Eighteen - Rhys

My relationship with Callum was complicated. It always would be, I knew that. But I didn't ever anticipate just how exhausting the travel could be during the rugby season. He had been commentating on a locum basis all around the country on the radio and TV, and with me playing matches almost every Saturday for Cardiff and training through the week, it felt harder and harder to keep any semblance of a steady relationship going. Travelling by train was time consuming and by air it was exhausting.

When we did see one another, it was still electric. Every time we touched I felt like I'd won the lottery. Every time he held my face in those big hands and kissed me, I wanted to never leave. But leave I did, every other week.

The sneaking around had started to grate on me too. I'd gone into the relationship with the knowledge that Callum wasn't out of the closet yet but I had forgotten just how tough that could be. We'd become more reclusive, almost always sticking to our homes in case a too-kind fan or paparazzi noticed that I was travelling from Cardiff to Edinburgh on a monthly basis, and he to me in reverse.

That had been partially fixed, but also exacerbated by the next shitty situation we found ourselves in. I'd been picked to play for Wales again in the Autumn Internationals, a series of matches in Cardiff against the best of the rest of the world. A gruelling schedule of weekly matches against Australia, New Zealand, South Africa, Argentina, Georgia and Fiji that took me out of regular action for Cardiff.

Because the training camp under Wesley was so intense, I was essentially confined to the Wales training hotel for six weeks. It was weird, having to room with George, a lovely winger with baby-face, rather than the company from Callum I'd gotten so used to. The training camp meant that Callum and I didn't have a chance to meet throughout November and into the start of December. When Sarah took on extra shifts at work and Callum then looked after his kids for the first two weeks of December, I felt like screaming up into the universe. I needed to feel his touch to remember he was real.

Finally, midway through December, I waited at Cardiff Central Station for Callum's train to come in. I was bouncing from foot to foot as I waited for him. I couldn't wait to hold him again. So much so that when he passed through the turnstiles I ran toward him and pulled him into a hug. He hugged me back for just a second before breaking away. No-one seemed to be paying us any attention, so I gestured for him to follow me out of the station.

He was wrapped up in big black coat and dark beanie because of the December weather. I could see his Cardiff Old Navy scarf just poking out from the edges of his collar.

"How was the journey?" I asked.

"Fucking shite," he laughed. "I wish I didn't have to come

CHAPTER EIGHTEEN - RHYS

down here all the time."

My step faltered for a second as Callum realised what he'd said. "No, not like that…"

"No, no. I get it." And I did. It just felt like Callum was worth the effort. I worried that at some point he'd feel like I wasn't worth the effort any more.

I shivered and blew warm air into my gloves, but my fingers were like icicles as we walked down Cardiff's St Mary Street. "Fancy a pint?" I asked.

"I'd love one," he said. We ducked into a nearby bar and sat in a shady table in the corner. He pulled off his hat, and his hair stuck up in every direction underneath.

"Cute," I said. I reached forward and rearranged his mussed up hair, pulling back when I noticed he'd frozen up.

"Sorry," I said.

"No. No worries." Silence fell between us again. "I'll get us a pint." He walked over to the bar, leaving me alone with my thoughts in the booth for a minute.

I hated not being able to show him affection at all when there might be people around. I knew I should have taken him straight to the flat where I could touch him all I liked, but having spent six weeks secluded in the training camp I wanted nothing more than to have a pint in the company of people. And it was starting to rankle, just a little bit, having to be so completely chaste around him when we were out and about. After weeks of not seeing one another I wanted to hold his hand, to give him a peck on the cheek in public. It felt sometimes like we were holding ourselves back from the things even *friends* might do out of fear of being seen as something more.

I thanked him as he put a pint of my favourite beer in front of me. "How's Finn?" he asked.

"He's good, I think. I've kept in contact via text and call. He's living back in the Valleys in his gran's old house."

"Wow." One of the titans of Welsh rugby, ending his career living in the back of beyond was a shock to anyone. But for Callum, who'd kept up his integrity for so long, it must have been unfathomable that someone could crash and burn so hard.

"It's…for the best, I think. Did you see the rest of the stuff?" I asked.

"Yup. People are pricks," Callum said. "I can't believe people were so determined to bring him down."

After the first video, the floodgates had opened. Finn hadn't been the most scrupulous in choosing his sexual partners or who he sent pictures and videos to. His irresponsibility had been his final downfall, but it still made my blood boil to think of people taking advantage of him like that. He might have been a bit of a party animal, but he never set out to hurt anyone.

"He's got an interview coming out in the next couple of days though, so that's good."

"Oh?" Callum asked.

"He wants to clear the air on his terms. Put his side out there. Plus an exclusive with *Sports Weekly* pays pretty well and he's very unemployed right now."

Callum laughed then sipped at his pint. "I feel sorry for the bugger, I really do. But good on him for moving on."

We finished our pints in silence. It felt like when we were around other people we couldn't even talk as friends, for fear something too close, too intimate, might slip out.

"Home?" I asked. Callum smiled.

We walked the five minutes from the pub to my flat through

CHAPTER EIGHTEEN - RHYS

the cold streets of Cardiff. It was a Friday and people were preparing to head out, just as we were heading in for the weekend.

"How's Sarah? And the kids?" I asked.

"They're great, they can't wait for Christmas," he said. "I'll go to Sarah's and stay in the spare room so they can open presents with us all together as a family. How about you?"

"I'm...good," I said. "I'll be...well, I'll be by myself Christmas morning. I'll head over to mum's in the afternoon though. That should be alright."

"Oh...good." The conversation served as just another reminder that our lives were so different sometimes. And that Callum's family would always be his first priority.

I unlocked the door to my flat and basked in the warmth for a second before I let Callum in. "Bloody lovely," I said, kicking my shoes off and unzipping my coat. Callum's hands were immediately on my face and he pulled me in for a kiss, our cold lips warming slowly as they worked as one.

"I've missed you," he said between kisses. "So, so much."

"Me too," I said. I grabbed at his scarf to keep his face close. "I wish we could do this every single day."

"You'd get bored of me pretty quickly," he said. "Though I have been learning some new tricks."

"Tricks?" I asked, ignoring the awkward self deprecation.

"Can I use your shower? I feel like I smell like train," he asked quickly.

"...sure." The abrupt change in conversation gave me whiplash but that was soon forgiven as Callum shamelessly stripped off completely in my hallway before heading to the shower. I nudged the balled up clothes into the corner and watched that toned rugby playing arse heading away.

"I hate that you leave, but I love to watch you go," I called after him. He just stuck his middle finger up at me without looking back. Maybe once he was out of the shower, we could talk about my worries about the future. Perhaps we'd talk the coming out plan.

I tidied up around the place whilst I waited from him to finish showering, and sat down on the sofa as I heard the water shut off. When Callum hadn't come back after five minutes, I wandered into the bedroom.

There he was, on my bed and completely naked, big furry rugby player legs pushed back and rubbing at his hole with one finger.

"Tricks," he said simply in explanation. "I wondered when you were going to come and find me."

I could feel myself getting hard in my trousers just at the sight of him, and sank to my knees at the edge of the bed, removing my t-shirt as I did so. With his legs held up high, I took his semi-hard cock and started to suck at the tip, even as he continued to reach below me to stroke at his hole. I choked myself down on him as I heard his moans getting louder.

"Do you want me inside of you?" I asked. I stroked Callum idly as I looked up at him. He nodded slowly, not saying a word.

This was…unfamiliar territory. I hadn't topped in a while, it was never my preference. But I wanted it to feel good for Callum. I sucked one finger into my mouth then used that finger to gently play with the puckered skin at his hole, a light pink patch of bare skin in amongst a smattering of light ginger hairs. It tightened reflexively at my touch, so I took his length into my mouth to give him some pleasure, some euphoria that would help him relax. I took all of his cock into my mouth in

CHAPTER EIGHTEEN - RHYS

one smooth motion, feeling him start to relax on my finger as I did.

I pushed gently at his entrance as I kept him distracted with my mouth. When his moans had reached a fever pitch and he was grasping at his thighs with white knuckles., I moved my attention downwards, licking down the length of him, then his balls, and finally to his puckered pink hole. Removing my finger, I licked over it and Callum shuddered. I kept my tongue flat as I passed over his hole again and again, slicking up the outside as he writhed and groaned at my attentions. I used my finger again, gaining easier entrance this time, and then tried another. He was tight and warm around my finger and he moaned as I brushed up against his prostate with two fingers. I looked up at Callum. His face was impassive but his eyes looking into mine with pure lust. "Lube?" I asked, and he passed me the tube he'd been using to prepare himself.

I coated my fingers with the lube and entered him again, giving a lick up his shaft as I did to keep him hard. "I need you to fuck me," he said.

"All in good time, love. I need to know you're ready." I hit his prostate with my fingers again and he squirmed.

"I've been practising...need it now..." he gasped.

"You really need it, do you?" I removed my fingers from him and slicked myself up with the lube.

"I do," he said. The intensity with which he looked at me made it clear that he was ready, whether I worried about him or not.

With the excess lube, I slicked up his cock and stroked him gently. I lowered my trousers to my knees as I stood at the edge of the bed to line myself up with his hole. I slid inside him slowly as he breathed out, still holding on to his own thighs.

Years of rugby training had made him flexible for his size, and I was surprisingly turned on by the thought of topping a man who could just as easily flip me back and have his way with me. Topping Callum, I felt like I was being allowed control rather than taking it for myself.

His channel was hot and tight round my cock as I sank to the hilt, and Callum smiled up at me with just a little sweat on his brow. "You really have been practising, haven't you?" I said.

"All the toys and six weeks without my boyfriend," he said, and I shuddered in pleasure at the thought of Callum speared on a dildo. I pulled back slowly until my cock was centimetres from sliding out of his hole, then slid back in just as slowly. We groaned in unison as I hit his sweet spot and he tightened around me.

"Go," he said. "I can take it."

I pulled back once more and pushed in, harder this time, my balls slapping against his skin as I pushed back in. Callum smiled blissfully and tipped his head back. Encouraged, I sped up my thrusts until we were both making noise in unison, his groans an octave higher than I was sued to and so sexy.

I stroked at his cock with my hand as he continued his white-knuckled grip on his own thighs. "I can't last like this," I said, feeling my own orgasm building and his cock twitching in my hand.

"Then don't," panted Callum. I leaned down between his thighs to kiss him as I pushed in and out of him, creating friction between his cock, my hand and our two bodies.

Our kissing became more frenzied until we were both just panting into one another mouths. I knew I was close. "Where do you want it?"

"Finish inside me…please," said Callum. That was enough

CHAPTER EIGHTEEN - RHYS

to finish me off and I shivered all over as I came into him with a shout. I thrust once, twice more and hard as I came. I felt his cum streaming over my fingers and heard him groan as he finished.

After a second, I withdrew from him slowly. Callum let go of his thighs and let them collapse onto the bed, red hand marks where he had been holding on so hard.

"Can we do that again?" he asked with cheeky grin.

"Play your cards right and make me a cup of tea and I might," I said. I collapsed next to him on the bed and gave him a very quick kiss.

19

Chapter Nineteen - Callum

"Four down, an expression of joy?" Rhys asked. He was sitting down on the other end of the sofa with a pencil between his teeth and his eyes on the newspaper in front of him. The only twenty-five year old in the world who still got the paper. He was still in his pyjamas but I was dressed after my morning run. For such an early riser, it could take a lot to get Rhys going in the mornings.

"Fuck?" I suggested. He just rolled his eyes.

"Ah…glee, maybe? I'll write it down for now." He did, gently with the pencil, rubber end at the ready in case he felt the need to completely change his answer later. "Oh! I didn't check the sports news! Did it come as well? I think Finn's interview will be in today's edition."

I reached over to the the paper on the counter that I'd grabbed when I headed out for our morning coffee. Finn's face took up most of the front page. He looked genuinely happy in the picture. *Telling My Truth*, said the headline beneath his chin. "He should get that framed," I mused. And then I felt my blood freeze as I noticed the pictures at the very bottom. Someone

CHAPTER NINETEEN - CALLUM

had captured a picture of the two of us at the train station locked in an embrace, and then another of Rhys reaching over to fix my messy hair in the pub. *Rugby Prince of Wales and The Retired Gentleman of Rugby Cosy Up over Pints.* "Fuck."

'What is it?" asked Rhys, snatching the paper from me and scanning the page. "Oh. That's fine though, right? It's not too mean or anything."

He flipped over to the page and read from it. Out loud. *"Wales' crowned Prince of Rugby, Rhys Prince, 25, was seen in Cardiff cosying up with its most recent eligible bachelor, Callum Anderson, 33...*not so bad, is it? They've not been cruel, and there's no mention of your sexuality...more gossip rag crap, I think. I can't believe they're printing any of this. It's a bit desperate for a sports paper to be writing gossip..."

I hardly heard him. "What if my kids see? My wife?" I asked. I caught Rhys' sharp intake of breath, and then he was at the side of the sofa with me.

"Hey, Sarah will understand, right? And she can help you explain it to the kids if..." Rhys tailed off for a second, as if he was realising that I was still frozen still. "...do you have *any* plans to tell them? Or anyone else?"

"I did, it's just..." I didn't know how to express what I was feeling to Rhys. The fear. The ever-present shame that still lingered over touches. "...I don't know how I can do it."

"Do what?" Rhys asked, voice low and controlled. There was so much fire bubbling underneath.

"...be gay." I finally spat out.

"Be gay?" Rhys asked, his voice raising ever so slightly. "What do you think you've been doing the last few months with me? Do you feel straight when you're fucking me? Did you feel straight last night when I was fucking you?"

"That's…not what I meant," I said. "I mean…I don't know how to be openly gay."

"I'm here to help you," Rhys started, but I cut him off before he could continue.

"I'm not sure I want to come out yet," I said.

Rhys kept his voice controlled. I was used to hearing him use this tone with Finn, when he went into help mode. "So when do you think you'll want to? In weeks? Years? I lo— I really like you, but I can't wait around for you forever, Cal."

Something in my heart twisted at the confirmation of what I had feared. "I wouldn't expect you to. I just…I don't know if I can give you what you want."

"Why, Callum? Are you ashamed of being with me? Or Is there something I've done, something I can do?"

"I'm not…ashamed of you," I said. "I'm ashamed…of me. And despite you being so wonderful, it's something I'm struggling to let go of. But seeing that article in the paper…I don't think I'm ready to face that kind of scrutiny yet."

"Scrutiny I've had since the say I started my career," Rhys said. "Scrutiny ten times less than what Finn has put himself through, with how he was forced out of the closet. All you'd need to do is hold my hand on the street, or kiss me after a match. Your secret would be out, and the world would move on."

"What if they don't? I asked. "What if they dredge up every time we've played against one another and spin it, like I've been cheating on my wife for years or…"

"Then we face it together," Rhys said. "Because that's what couples do."

"I don't deserve you," I said. My heart was heavy as horrific, and tempting, intrusive thoughts ran through my head. *I could*

CHAPTER NINETEEN - CALLUM

make this so much easier for Rhys.

"What are you trying to say?" he asked.

"I…don't know. I really like being with you, but I just…I can't be with you and promise you I'm ever going to come out."

"Well that's fine, we can work something out," said Rhys, holding my arm as if I was already moving away from him.

"Can you honestly tell me you'd be happy with me not being out? With you never being able to hold my hand in the street? Waving off questions whenever a sports or LGBT site asks about your relationship status?" I asked. I was sabotaging myself and I knew it. I just hoped that at some point I'd be able to forgive myself for it. For letting go.

"Then what do you want?" Rhys asked after a moment.

"I…it's not about what I want, is it?" I asked, my voice coming out sharper than intended.

"Well it certainly doesn't seem to be about what I fucking want does it?" he said.

I couldn't think of anything to say, so I slowly gathered my composure before standing up to leave. "I should go."

Rhys didn't reply. Didn't look me in the eye as I grabbed my suitcase from the hallway and opened the door. When I looked back, he wasn't looking at me. He faced away from me, staring at the patio doors as I left.

20

Chapter Twenty - Rhys

It was only half an hour before a key turned in the lock and Mum rushed into the flat. I was letting the tears flow freely and she looked at me with pity in her eyes I hadn't seen since the day I came out to her at fourteen.

"Oh, love. What's happened now?" she was at my side and pulling my head to her shoulder in seconds. I dampened the wool of her cardigan with my tears for a few more minutes before I could give her an answer.

"Just…just a man," I said.

"I've never known you to be so hung up on *just a man* before. C'mon, whose door do I have to knock? It's been a whole since I've thrown a punch but I can tell you they used to fear me in the Corporation Pub back in the day."

"Doesn't matter, mam," I said. I still owed it to Callum to protect his identity, but Mum was reaching for the ripped up copy of the sports paper on the floor. "Oh, love. Married?"

I shrugged before letting out another sob and she rubbed my back. "Tea? Or something stronger?" she asked.

"Just a tea, Mam." She threw the mugs Callum and I had

CHAPTER TWENTY - RHYS

been using less than an hour before into the sink and started making the tea with fresh cups. "So. How long has this been going on?"

"About four months," I answered honestly.

"And you were…serious…about him?"

I nodded, not trusting the lump in my throat not to stop me from speaking. She carried the mugs over to the coffee table and started to clear up the mess.

"So he ended things, why? Did his wife find out? Were you going behind her back. You know I'm not one for judgement but…"

I snorted through the tears. If only God could judge then on a Saturday night in the local Bingo Hall my mum was very much a god. "No, she knew. He's that Scottish one, the one who separated a few months back."

"The retired one? Wait, didn't you used to have pictures of him on your walls? He's a bit old for you, isn't he?"

"I thought we weren't judging?" I asked.

"Well I'm not but if I'd known you were going for older men I'd have asked Harold at the Bingo if he was interested."

Mum sounded so earnest that I had to laugh. "There's a difference between thirty-three and sixty-three, Mam."

"Well I'm glad it got you smiling." Mam took a sip of her tea and looked over the mug at me. "What are you going to do now?"

"Same as ever, I suppose. Keep playing rugby and being bloody good at it," I said. I wiped at the snot under my nose with my sleeve, already starting to feel gross for how much I'd cried and let myself go.

"I worry about you," Mam said. "Always so hushed up with your emotions. You've managed to keep a four month relationship from your own mother…how can I know that you're actually OK? That you're not going to…I don't know, throw yourself over the balcony tomorrow?"

"I'll get some goldfish," I said. "Can't kill myself if I have goldfish."

Mum looked horrified and I remembered that Gen-Z humour probably wouldn't land so much with her. "Sorry Mam, I mean to say…that I'll talk to you if I'm down. See? Already over him. Men are gross. I should have just been straight. See? Easy."

My lame attempts at humour weren't going down well at all. "Just…take care of yourself, OK?"

I could already feel the next wave of tears welling up and I took a generous slurp of hot tea to distract myself. "I will," I said.

Chapter Twenty-One - Callum

I looked at the front door for a second after I'd rung the bell, wondering why I'd even bothered coming here immediately after getting off the train. I still had a key, but this was Sarah's house now. Not mine. I had a compulsion to see her and the kids, and I thought I knew why. Because I'd abandoned one of the people I loved I needed reassurance that the other three were still there, as they always would be.

When the door opened, I knew then I definitely shouldn't have come. Because it wasn't Sarah at the door, but the Monster in Law. "Hi, Elizabeth," I said. "Is Sarah in?"

"She should be home from work in about five minutes. Here to see the kids? It's been a while."

"I've been looking after them for the last two weeks, Elizabeth. We do have a shared custody agreement."

"Hm." Elizabeth didn't seem to agree with my appraisal of the situation but stood aside anyway as I came in.

I could hear the sound of shooting and screaming going on in the front room so I went in immediately. The kids seemed to be engaged in a fire-fight with some gruesome looking zombies and blood splattered the screen as Logan's character died. He covered his head with the pillow and screamed. "Turn it off, Liv! Turn it off!"

"Stop being such a baby," his sister said.

"I really think you should turn that off," I said. Sometimes I forgot how the scary dad-voice came out on instinct. Both kids immediately turned to me. Logan was still shaking and Olivia's face turned down at the edges. She immediately reached for the TV remote and switched it off. Once the TV was off, I walked past them both to pull the XBOX lead out from the socket and wrapped it around my arm. "Who said you could play this kind of game?" I asked.

Both sets of eyes turned to the door, to where Elizabeth was standing, hands on her hips and looking completely unrepentant. "Want to have a talk?" I asked her.

"Gladly," she replied. She walked toward the kitchen with the expectation I'd follow her. *Why do all the confrontations in this house take place in the bloody kitchen?* I asked myself. "Right both, have you got homework to be doing before your mum gets home?" Two heads nodded slowly. I held up the wire from the console. "If you get to it before your mum gets home, I'll think about letting you have the console back before tonight."

They both scampered up the stairs, and I took a deep breath toward where I could hear Elizabeth clattering away with pots and pans in the kitchen.

She was placing a lasagne on the heat mat in the middle of the kitchen island when I walked in, the image of a kind and doting grandmother. I held up the cable as I had when I was talking to the kids.

"Want to explain?" I asked.

"Lasagne?" she countered, scooping out a piece and putting

CHAPTER TWENTY-ONE - CALLUM

it on a plate. It looked bloody lovely, but I wasn't in the mood to be distracted by such an ill-thought out peace offering. "Not hungry."

"Suit yourself. The children should be coming down to tea right now," she said.

"They're doing the homework they already should have been doing," I countered.

"Well I am their grandmother and..."

"And I am their father," I said, cutting her off. "And I've no idea why a lady of your age, who once told me that playing silly games would make their eyes go all funny, is suddenly in possession of a zombie game. Because it certainly isn't Sarah's, and I don't remember buying it for the kids."

"Well I thought they could do with something new to try," she said innocently, dishing out lasagne perfectly on each plate in turn.

"And you cleared it with Sarah?" I asked, wondering for the first time if my anger was misplaced.

"A grandmother should be able to make some decisions in her own grandchildren's lives, surely? Especially when I've taken care of them so much over the years."

Every time I spoke to Elizabeth it made my head ache. But today it was like being jabbed with a million tiny needles, like if she spoke to me long enough she might just actually drive me insane.

"And your decision was to let Logan, an eleven year old boy, play on an eighteen rated game when you know he cries at the sight of gore?"

"Well he needed toughening up," Elizabeth said passively. She filled herself a glass of water from the jug in the fridge.

"And what exactly is that supposed to mean?" I asked. "What

does Logan need toughening up from?"

"Well, he's just so…" Elizabeth started. I waited for her to finish, unwilling to speak for fear of what I might say to her that I couldn't take back.

"Just so what?" asked Sarah from the doorway. Both Elizabeth and I jumped like we'd been stung as we turned to look at her, hands on her hips in a way that looked so like her mother. But her anger was directed at the woman herself, and Elizabeth seemed to lose a bit of her confidence.

"Just…so…sensitive," said Elizabeth slowly. "Sarah, I didn't hear you come in! Lasagne?"

"Someone left the front door open," said Sarah. "So what is it about your own grandson that you felt the need to toughen him up?" She took a step closer to her mother, and I took a step back. I had never seen the two fight and I was almost scared to see it now.

"Well…you see," Elizabeth glanced toward me. "I've heard it runs in the family, and I didn't want…"

"Didn't want what?" Sarah asked. "You thought because my husband turned out gay that my own son would? You thought sweet, sensitive Logan might be corrupted into femininity by my rugby playing husband?"

"I just…I was doing what was best!" Elizabeth exploded. "You know he's going to get bullied at school, the way he is! He's too sensitive to stand up to bullies and you know it! He needs to survive in the real world!"

I finally found my voice. "And shooting games are how he's going to do that, are they?"

"Well I couldn't exactly encourage him into rugby, could I?" Elizabeth muttered. "That never helped you."

"Out." Sarah said. "I will talk to you when I have the strength

CHAPTER TWENTY-ONE - CALLUM

to talk to you, Mum. But until I ask for you to come back, I don't want you back. I wanted someone who could care for my kids when I needed them to. If you can't love them unconditionally then I do not want you here at all."

"But..." Elizabeth started, but Sarah took the plate of lasagne from her and pointed to the door.

"Out," she repeated, and Elizabeth stalked out. Once we heard the front door close behind her, some of the tension left the room and we both slumped. "Wine?" Sarah asked, and I nodded.

"Thanks for saving me there," I said.

"No worries. My mother is a piece of work, but you know that already. And she has her uses when it comes to looking after the kids at least."

"Well I was always off with the rugby teams," I said. "But I'm home now. If you want your mother less involved in our kids' lives then I am here to take on the extra burden."

Sarah passed a big measure of white wine over to me, and I took a gulp. What Sarah didn't know is that Elizabeth had spoken to my very biggest fear. That who I was could lead to Logan being ostracised, alone. And I wasn't going to let that happen.

Even if my heart ached for Rhys.

Chapter Twenty-Two - Rhys

It was New Year's Day, and Cardiff Old Navy were in Edinburgh for the rugby. I loved the city normally, but I had walked straight from the team bus to the hotel, slept the night and stepped back onto the team bus to take me to the stadium. I was glad Callum had retired, because the thought of seeing his face was…not good. I had been holding it together for three weeks admirably but I wasn't about to let seeing him break that composure.

So what if I had actually bought goldfish? The tank was a nice addition to the flat and their personalised *Don't Jump Off The Balcony* ornament had gone down so badly with my mother that she'd stayed on the sofa for two nights afterwards to keep an eye on me. I was surprised she hadn't stolen the keys to my balcony door.

But I'd made it through a couple of matches, then Christmas and now the trip to Edinburgh without crying at anyone. Which was good, because in my private moments I was a fucking *mess*.

Edinburgh's home stadium was a little bigger than the Arms

CHAPTER TWENTY-TWO - RHYS

Park and the changing rooms definitely smelled nicer. We all got a pep talk off the boss before running out on the pitch to cheers from the Cardiff fans who had travelled all the way up to watch us play.

The game was a subdued one - the post-Christmas games often were and the stadium wasn't full to bursting like it would be at the very start of the season and for the final. A narrow loss to Edinburgh Thistle was enough to add to my already foul mood. When everyone else had left the changing room, I was still showering. The kit boys would be around later to wash the kits but in the moment I was by myself. And I needed that.

I let the searing hot spray turn my skin red as I stood underneath. I'd been at the gym every day since Callum and I had called it quits, and my body was feeling tight. I closed my eyes for a second, just allowing myself to imagine his smile, the way his eyes crinkled at the sides with crow's feet when he laughed.

And that deep, Scottish brogue saying, "I'm sorry."

My eyes snapped open. Because that hadn't been in my imagination. In front of me, stood in the archway between the shower blocks and the changing rooms, was Callum. He was wearing his Cardiff Old Navy scarf and that big black coat, and twiddling a small box wrapped in gold between his two palms. "I'm sorry," he repeated.

My heart was pounding in my chest at the earnest way he said it, the way he looked at me with sadness in those big beautiful eyes. I wanted to tell him it was all OK, that I could forgive him. But for what?

"For what?" I echoed my thoughts.

"For...everything. For breaking your heart. I don't know

why I did it, now. I wish I'd just…I wish I'd been more of a coward. I wish I'd been selfish, and put my own feelings first. Being without you *hurts*."

I knew it hurt. I hurt. But I knew that the last couple of weeks standing as strong as I could could not be for nothing. I couldn't go through that intense, heart-rending pain that the moment of losing him had given me. "Well, it's too late, isn't it?" I said. "You've done it now. And it's not exactly the kind of thing you can take back."

I turned the shower tap off, then stepped around him and into the changing room. I was doing my best to keep my face impassive as I did. He didn't deserve my emotion.

I dried off and got dressed as quickly as I could, aware of his eyes on my back the whole time. Once I was fully dressed and my kit had been thrown into the corner with everyone else's, I turned back to face Callum. He had taken a step closer to me whilst my back was turned, and I looked up into his eyes.

"What do you want from this?" I asked. "Want us to go back to how we were? Sneaking around, just like you said you couldn't let me do any more? Or would you rather actually come out with it all?"

Callum was silent but I watched a tear escape from one eye. I took a step closer to him so we were within touching distance. I hated hurting him, but he had been right. Him not coming out would hurt me in the long run, no matter how I felt. I held out one hand, and he reached for it, but I pulled back before could touch me.

"Really think about this," I said, then nodded at the closed door to the changing rooms. "If someone walks right through that door right now, a match official, referee, player or coach. Would you be happy caught holding hands with me?"

CHAPTER TWENTY-TWO - RHYS

After a moment of hesitation Callum withdrew his hand. "No," he said. "And I hate myself for that. It's my dream to hold hands with you in public. To kiss you on the rugby pitch with everyone watching. But that's all it is. A dream. I don't know that I can ever give you that."

"And why is that? You trying to shield yourself from scrutiny? From not looking like the Gentleman of Rugby?"

"No...my...my kids," he said. I could see I was breaking him and every word out of my mouth felt so painful but so necessary.

"Tell me now, if Logan or Olivia came out tomorrow, would you want them to live out and proud? Or would you expect them to hide too? Because you don't have to come out, Cal. No one can make you. But if you're worried about setting an example for your kids? Then hiding is the wrong answer. Now, if we're done...I have to go. Please don't do this to me again."

A hand reached out and grabbed my arm. I turned to face him. In his other hand, he held the little wrapped box. "For Christmas," he said. "I...I need you to have it."

I took the gift gingerly like it could burn me, and ran from the changing room before he could see me lose it. I hated that I had come round to Callum's logic just as he decided it didn't matter. We were like two broken clocks, never quite on the right time as one another. Never quite ticking at the same pace. And as much as I felt like my heart was going to rip itself out of my chest and run back to him. I forged onwards.

The team bus sat silent and dark in the car park as the team had decided to head to the nearest rugby club for a commiserating pint. I walked through Edinburgh's cold, brisk night to the hotel. The wrapped box felt cold in my hand and

I was half-tempted to throw it away before I could look at it. Surely I should, to avoid the inevitable heartbreak when I was reminded of just how thoughtful Callum could be?

I opened my room door with one shaking swipe of the card on the reader and then walked slowly over to the bed. I sat down on it, and held the present out in front of me. I could leave it and never know exactly what it held. What was worse? Never knowing what Callum's last gift to me was, never getting the closure? Or the heartbreak of that very same closure?

I pulled apart the wrapping. Inside was a small black jewellery box and my heart leapt out of my chest as I considered the possibility that it might be a ring. But Callum wasn't the kind of guy to rub this in my face...was he? Was he so desperate to take me back that he would apologise even as I was dissecting our relationship in a gruesome post-mortem?

Hands hardly able to hold onto the box, I opened it at the hinge and brought one hand to my mouth. Inside the box and nestled in velvet was a necklace, a simple thick gold chain with two tiny jewelled ornaments threaded on. A tiny sapphire-tinted ship and an amethyst flower. A Navy vessel and a thistle. Our two teams, entwined on the very same necklace.

I resisted the urge to throw the whole thing away. It was thoughtful, kind and so completely Callum.

I took off my hoodie and jeans, my shoes and socks, and placed them all on the floor next to my bed. I took the necklace from its box and clasped it around my neck before laying down in bed, reaching for the switch to turn off the lights.

Hours later, my room-mate burst into the room after a night of heavy drinking. I laid still and pretended to be asleep. Under the covers, I clutched at the reminders of the relationship I loved. I didn't get a second of sleep all night.

23

Chapter Twenty-Three - Callum

Logan and Olivia for once were united in their interests as they sang the world's most out of key rendition of *Let it Go* from *Frozen*. I was minutes away from Sarah's house and though I was an hour early, I was hoping she would be up for a cup of coffee and a chat.

Because I was hurting, and had been for the best part of three months. Valentine's Day was coming up and Rhys Prince was still on my brain. He was always on my mind, these days.

We had texted a little bit back and forth as he thanked me for my present. A week later, a Cardiff Old Navy shirt with *Anderson* on the back had arrived in the post for me.

Otherwise, I'd sent the odd text letting him know I'd seen how well he was playing for both Cardiff and Wales, and he had responded with polite, if distant replies.

"The cold never bothered me anyway!" Logan finished with a flourish as I turned off the car. I'd bought him an Elsa wand from the theatre the night before and he was loving the chance to wave it anywhere and anytime that he could.

I got out of the car just as Sarah's front door opened and

a man who looked to be in his forties, dressed in casual of expensive clothes, stepped out. As soon as he saw me, he hurried over to his car and got in without a word. Sarah stood on the doorstep in her pyjamas, face unreadable, as I got the kids out of the car as soon as I'd seen he was gone.

"Time for a cuppa?" I asked her with a wry smile. Sarah rolled her eyes and gestured for me to step inside. I ushered the kids in first and both gave her a hug before running up to their rooms. They had lots of things in my new flat, but a week without their games consoles was enough to drive them insane.

We walked to the kitchen and Sarah flicked on the kettle before turning to look at me. We both stared for a very long time, like a good old fashioned Mexican stand-off.

"Fine," she finally said as she spooned sugar into the mugs so she didn't have to look at me. "His name is Clive, he's a consultant at the hospital…and about two months. He hasn't met the kids yet."

"Serious?" I asked. She passed me the coffee and I lifted it to smell. I'd gone off tea since Rhys and I had split. It felt weird drinking it to de-stress without him now.

"I think so. He's really nice, Callum. I know this must be weird for you…" she paused as if waiting for some kind of approval, or for me to throw all my toys out of the pram at the thought of her with someone else.

"I'm happy for you, honest."

Sarah's mouth split into a smile. "Thank god for that. It's weird telling your own husband that you're seeing someone new."

"Ex-husband," I corrected. "Seriously. It's good to see you happy."

CHAPTER TWENTY-THREE - CALLUM

"Are you, though?" Sarah asked. "I know you don't like to talk about him, but are you happy? You know I'm thrilled that you've moved on, it was just all of a bit of a shock."

"We...broke up." I should have known that asking Sarah to talk about her relationship could lead to this.

"Why?" Sarah took a sip of her coffee. "Twenty-five too young for you?"

"Twenty six now, actually," I said before I could stop myself. "Anyway, no, it's not that."

"What then? God knows he's young and gorgeous enough. Do you know how inadequate it makes a woman feel when her husband decides his first post-divorce relationship is going to be Wales' most gorgeous rugby prodigy? Did he think you were too *old?*"

"No, Sar. I just...I can't be what he needs. I can't come out. I don't want the papers speculating that I was cheating on you, or the kids to get bullied in school because their dad is a poof."

"I don't think I've heard the word poof since about 2003, and I think it was you saying it. So I don't think that's a worry," Sarah laughed to herself.

"I'm serious!" I protested.

"No, you're not." Sarah pointed vaguely upwards at the ceiling. "Logan is already obsessed with Disney princesses and musicals. Do you think school is going to be easy for him either way? I've agonised over whether I should talk to him before he starts high school, tell him to tone it down. But I don't think I could bear it. I cannot bear the thought of our son having to change himself for anyone. So I will support him however he expresses himself. My mother will not dampen his spirit and you can bet that no one else will either."

If you're worried about setting an example for your kids? Then hiding is the wrong answer. The memory of my last conversation with Rhys was seared into my brain. Was I coward for hiding from them as well as the world?

"How the hell do I come out to our kids, Sar? How do you drop a bombshell like that?"

"Probably just by saying the words out loud, I should imagine," said Sarah. "They learn about all this at school now, it's not like we're introducing them to the concept."

"What, just…Logan, Olivia, daddy fancies men now? Like that?"

"Daddy?" a voice from behind me made me freeze, but Sarah smirked.

"Just like that," she said.

I turned slowly to face my two kids in the doorway. "You…fancy men," asked Olivia. "Really?"

I let out a breath. I couldn't tell what either of them was thinking. They were silhouetted in the light of the hallway and I was scared to take a step toward them. "Yes," I finally said. "I'm…"

"Gay?" Logan suggested. "Because we learned about all that stuff weeks ago!" He rushed forward and enveloped my stomach in a hug.

Olivia shrugged from the doorway and took the steps needed to join Logan in the hug. I felt tears prick at the back of my eyes. "If you have to be with a man, can you find one who's good at DIY?" she asked. "Because my bookshelves have been wonky for ages but I knew you couldn't fix it."

I choked back a laugh and a sob at the same time. "I love you both, so much."

"Are you…are you going to start dancing and drama now, Dad? Because that's what they do on that old show mum was

CHAPTER TWENTY-THREE - CALLUM

watching on Netflix the other day…" Logan sounded doubtful, and I realised what he was doing. He was worried if I acted like him, then that might make him gay. Like because he fit all the stereotypes then he would be lumped in with me.

I extracted myself from the hug and crouched down to hold one of their hands in each of mine. "I am already a *fantastic* dancer," I said. Sarah laughed behind me but I ignored her. "But that doesn't make me gay. Neither of you has to follow the path people have set for you. If either of you wants to be a rugby player, a ballet dancer, a princess. Then follow your dreams and don't you ever worry that what you do will make people think you have to fancy a certain gender. Be who you want to be, and don't let anyone else define you."

"No offence Dad, but that was really cringe," said Olivia. She was smiling though, and I knew she was OK. I gave them both a watery smile.

"I need to talk to your mum for a minute," I said. "Want to go and set up Switch Sports and I'll join you for some bowling in a minute?"

Both kids ran off without another word. "Didn't you take them bowling this weekend? And the weekend before?"

"I know, very Sunday dad of me but they want to go all the time and I can't say no." I hesitated before continuing. "Thank you. For making that easier."

"You just needed a little push," she said. "You're a good man, Cal. You just need to see it. If you want to chase the man of your dreams then I have no objection to that as long as the kids remain your first priority. And with the way you are as a dad, I know they always will be. I don't care what the papers or gossips say. I want me, you and the kids to live the most authentic lives we can. And I think you were using as a crutch because you're too afraid of coming out."

She was right, I knew she was. "So," I said. "How do I do it?"

"Come out, get the man of your dreams, ride off happily into the sunset?" she asked. "I don't know. I've never come out as gay and I have no plans to any time soon."

"Lucky Clive," I said. She leaned over to punch me in the arm.

"Be serious for a sec. What does Rhys want? And what do you want? Because as weird as it is, I'm determined to see you happy with someone." Sarah pulled out a pen and paper from one of the kitchen drawers.

I tried my best to gather the words. I knew Rhys so well, every part of him and every little flaw. I knew him on the rugby pitch and in the bedroom, and I knew how his face scrunched up with concentration at the morning crossword. But what did he want? he'd told me.

"He wants someone to love him openly, with no holds barred. He's put so much time into playing rugby, and all that time he's been open about who he is. He wants…no, he deserves to be with someone who can be open about how much they love him. He deserves everything. I can't for a second give him everything he deserves, but I'm willing to try."

"And what do you want?" Sarah rubbed at a tear under her eye before she put the pen back on the paper.

"I want him to love me back. That's all I need."

"Then let's work out how you're going to get that to happen."

Chapter Twenty-Four - Rhys

I strapped on my boots for our second game of the year against Edinburgh. This time, we were at home, and the atmosphere was in our favour. After our narrow loss and the aftermath last time, this game felt personal to me.

I smiled over at George, who had moved from his squad in England to Cardiff to facilitate better training with Wales in future. He was a cheeky, slightly chubby guy and I sensed flirtatious vibes from him, but it was just nice to have a good friend on the squad again since Finn had left. I checked my phone. Finn had texted to let me know he was sitting down in the stands, ready for the game ahead. I was looking forward to seeing him again after the game.

"Right, we've got typical Welsh weather," said Garrett as he gathered us for a pre-match pep talk. "Which means it's fucking pouring, boys. If we were playing football we'd be called off. But rugby is a man's sport!"

I roared along with the rest of the team even as it made me want to roll my eyes. Garrett was an old-fashioned coach considering he was only in his thirties. I was starting as a flanker as usual, and the team were amped up despite the weather. Bernie, our match physio, was fluttering around us to make sure no last-minute injuries were going to crop up.

We stepped from the tunnel as one team, and let the roar of seven thousand fans engulf us and spur us on. It was time to get to work.

The rain really was pouring down, the mid-February weather really letting loose on Cardiff. It was my last game before I would head back to the hotel in Glamorgan for the Wales training camp for my second Six Nations. It was time to show these Scots what they would be facing from me on the international stage.

My style of rugby was hard to transfer to the weather we were playing in. I was a fast runner and the ground was slippery, making it hard to swerve and dodge. I had to play more confrontational rugby, and trust that the Goliaths around me were going to be even more screwed up by the slipperiness of the pitch. As soon as I had the ball I charged headstrong into the Edinburgh defensive line, offloading to our number ten, who ran and scored our first try. As much as I loved to bask in the glory of a try, I was there to play for the team.

It was strange playing against Edinburgh without Callum there. As our kicker lined himself up for a two-point conversion I shook my head. I had spent the best part of three months moping over Callum. I still wasn't over him, but I sure as hell could put him out of my mind for one game.

The rain was causing puddles on the pitch, and with the floodlights on the ground I could hardly even see the crowds. They were just a wall of sound whenever we got close to the touchline.

The game felt long and desperate as the rain blinded us,

CHAPTER TWENTY-FOUR - RHYS

covered us in mud and gunk with every try and made every push for a try feel more like a wrestling match with an octopus than a rugby game. When the whistle finally blew for half-time, we were one conversion — just two points — ahead of Edinburgh Thistle. We trooped off into the relative warmth of the changing rooms.

"Come on, boys! This is our home ground! Our weather!" Garrett shouted into the room as many of us changed into dry kits. It felt like I was at risk of hypothermia as I shivered in my new slightly damp kit, boxers still soaked and plastered to my thighs. I rubbed at most of the mud with a towel knowing I was probably making the problem worse.

I risked a quick check of my phone as Garrett carried on with the pep talk.

Finn: You're playing amazing - glad I brought my anorak, though, the stadium is leaky as fuck. Can't believe you're playing against Callum's team with him in the dugout!

What? Callum in the stands? I put my phone back in my bag, swallowing my heart as it threatened to erupt from my mouth. Why was he watching? He wasn't part of the team, not even on the coaching staff as far as I was aware from my late-night scrolling to find out what he was up to.

I took a swig of an energy drink before we ran out to still my shaking hands. Callum or no Callum, I was here to beat Edinburgh Thistle. For anyone else, having their ex in the stands should be a motivation to do better. I knew I had to pummel their side now, no mercy. No weakness. I would show him how well I was doing, and then maybe — and it broke my heart to even think about it — we could move on. Maybe I could find someone else who made me feel that way.

You fool. I knew I wouldn't. Callum was something special.

The ball was kicked high into the air at the ref's whistle and despite positioning myself right under it I fumbled it and knocked it forward into one of the opposing players' way. He took it and barged right through our defensive line, scoring a try for Edinburgh.

As their kicker lined himself up with the ball I sidled over towards the dugout. Through the rain and brightness of the floodlights the figures inside resolved themselves into the recognisable shapes of people. Edinburgh's eight substitute players, some of the coaching staff...and Callum. Watching me intently with big blue eyes, and despite his position in his old team's dugout he was still wearing that stupid Cardiff scarf under his coat.

He nodded at me with a small smile on his face, and I immediately ran away. *Coward.* But I couldn't face him now. I needed to play, and make up for my stupid mistake. And I would decide on how best - or if, to confront Callum later.

We lined ourselves up to start again, and our kicker started the game off. This time, I rushed toward the Edinburgh players and managed to tackle their player as soon as he had the ball. He offloaded the ball to his teammate but I'd already stalled their momentum by rushing them. Further down the line, George ripped the ball from one of their players and ran to score a try. When our player missed the following conversion, we were at equal scores.

"Come on boys!" I shouted down the line as Edinburgh's kicker started us off. The clock was ticking down slowly toward the eighty minute mark and I was determined that we eke out a win.

CHAPTER TWENTY-FOUR - RHYS

The ball was in our hands straight away, but it was a slow and horrible push to the line through the mud and the rain. As our players wrestled further down the line with their Scottish opposition, obscured by rain and drowning in mud, some instinct told me to hold back. To keep myself separate from the pack.

And then the ball was loose from the maul and sailing towards me. I plucked it from the air and ran towards the wide open gap in Edinburgh's defence. Somehow, the slippery mud and grass worked to my advantage as I dodged one Edinburgh player's grabbing hands as another slipped off my slick arms like I was covered in oil. The try line was in sight, and I could hear the splashing of feet so close behind me as I dived with the ball into the muddy mess, placing the ball just over the line. The ref's whistle blew and I was swept up into the team's huddle before I could even stand by myself. The crowd was screaming my name and singing along to Tom Jones.

It didn't matter if we made the kick now, with seventy-nine minutes on the clock we were guaranteed the win. As the time ticked past eighty minutes and the kicker finally took his kick, sailing it over the crossbar, the crowd erupted into something crazy. The rain hadn't dampened their spirits and with a win under our belt it wasn't bothering us either. We all celebrated for a minute, one muddy and gross mass of men, before heading over to the opposition team. I shook hands with each of their players in turn as their bench of substitutes and coaching staff emerged into the rain to shake our hands too.

I watched that dugout bench as Callum stood up and brushed his hands off before stepping out into the pouring rain. He didn't shake hands with any other player, just headed straight for me. His features came into sharp focus under the bright white floodlights as the rain poured down on each of us. His skin looked stark white in the light and the rain had plastered his orange hair onto his face. He had a smattering of stubble, orange with little points of grey, and his eyes looked the brightest blue I had ever seen them. He smiled even as I stood still and let him approach.

"Hey, you," he mouthed. He took my hand and shook it, but held it there for a moment longer.

"What are you doing here?" I asked him. I could sense the whole crowd going quiet as we stood in silence.

"I want you," he said, and I felt my heart constrict. *I can't do this again*, I thought. *I cannot keep up this ridiculous charade with a man who won't even leave the closet door slightly ajar.*

I moved to pull away, but his hand's grip was firm on mine. "Let me go," I said, my words laced with the double meaning.

"I will," he said, "if you're willing to listen for a second. I want you…and I don't care who knows."

For just a second I let myself hope. Let myself think that he might stick to that promise. But he had left before, hadn't he? "Prove it."

"How?" he asked.

"You…you told me your dream, the one you couldn't have. You wanted to kiss me on the rugby pitch. You told me you wished that we could be that open about our relationship. But you couldn't. Prove to me that you want to be with me."

Callum leaned back for a second, his hand dropped mine, and I was vindicated even as my heart tore into tiny little pieces. But then that same hand looped round my waist and pulled me closer. "Is that what you want?" he asked.

"Yes," I whispered, and then his lips were on mine in front

CHAPTER TWENTY-FOUR - RHYS

of seven thousand spectators. His mouth parted mine as we kissed, rain making our face set and slippery. And just for a second I didn't care. And then I remembered where we were. The crowd was silent as I pulled away from Callum but his hand stayed at my waist.

Other than the sound of the rain splashing into puddles at our feet, the silence in the stadium was intense. And then there was one clap from somewhere high in the stands. Seconds later came another, then another, quicker and quicker until I could hear the whole stadium in applause. Callum gave a cheery wave as I stood stock still. Who was this man so confident in his sexuality and where had he come from?

"I'll meet you at the flat," he said, and then he was striding away through the rain toward the Edinburgh dugout until he was just a shadow in the lights. All that kept me from realising that it wasn't a dream was the taste of him on my lips.

There was a clap on my back and I looked up at George, who was stood with a wide grin on his face. I didn't know what the kiss from Callum had really meant, but I knew that it had meant a seismic shift in everything we were.

25

Epilogue

Callum

The crowd was roaring at Murrayfield Stadium, and for once I wasn't on the pitch to play or to help newer players understand the atmosphere and plays. I was here to talk about rugby. The build-up in the stadium was electric.

My fellow pundit, Gavin, an ex-Wales player, had made me feel right at home in the stands with a mic as we spoke to Annie, the BBC's foremost rugby presenter.

"So, boys, who are you hoping is going to win today?" she asked.

"Wales, obviously," said Gavin. "Though with how Scotland are playing they've got their work cut out for them."

"And you, Callum? I imagine the decision is going to be made rather more difficult by your association with a certain Welsh player..." Annie's words were laced with double meanings, but I'd known the question was going to come up.

"My old, patriotic heart is with Scotland. But of course I hope Rhys plays well for Wales," I said. "He's going to be Scotland's biggest threat as they just don't have anyone as fast as him."

EPILOGUE

"Not showing any bias there?" she asked.

"Come on," replied Gavin. "He's right. No player can match Rhys Prince for speed. He's like a whippet."

"Thank you, that's all we have time for. Please join us for more coverage at half-time." Annie dismissed us both with a wave of her hand and the production team took our microphones.

"Thanks for that," I said. "I knew the question as coming but I didn't know she'd push it."

"No worries," said Gavin. We both walked down toward the seats that had been reserved for us in amongst the players' families and friends. "You were right. But then I guess you'd know all about how fast Rhys Prince is." He waggled his eyebrows suggestively and I cuffed him on the arm. Gavin was old-school Welsh rugby - tough, no-nonsense and nothing was off limits. I was just glad he hadn't said it in front of the cameras.

I took a seat between Finn Roberts and my kids. "They were great, no trouble at all," said Finn. I wouldn't have trusted him before but something seemed to have changed in him. He seemed more put-together than I'd ever known him but still hadn't started playing for Cardiff or Wales again.

"Finn let me have a sip of his beer!" Logan said with a smile, dispelling any notion I had of Finn as a responsible adult. I looked at him with my best *I am a Dad* face and he just laughed.

"Tell me you weren't drinking beers in the park by thirteen," Finn said.

"He's eleven!" I countered.

"Start 'em early, that's what I always say," he grinned.

"Idiot."

"Can I have a beer, Dad? Finn just said *you* were drinking at thirteen," Olivia asked slyly.

"Behave and you can have a sip of shandy. *At home.*" I added as Finn went to pass his drink over to my thirteen year old daughter. He grinned sheepishly.

Behind us, Garrett Gray and Wesley Peterson were gossiping like two old women. Wesley had announced his retirement not long after me, and was taking Wales through this one last Six Nations tournament. Garrett was lined up as his replacement, being promoted from head Coach of Cardiff's club team to Wales' regional team. Finn kept glancing over his shoulder at Garrett. For some reason Bernie, Cardiff's physio, was here too, pacing behind Garrett and muttering to himself.

The whistle blew, and the game started. And I only had eyes for one man on that team.

Rhys played like a whirlwind. He said he had always looked up to me. Well now, in my retirement, I could say I looked up to him. He was a legend of the British game already. I wanted people to forget I had ever played, wanted every eye in the stadium just on him. If his bright light made the rest of us look dim in comparison, then he deserved it.

"Is Uncle Rhys staying over tonight?" Logan asked.

"I don't know how many times, Logan. He's not your uncle. He's Daddy's boyfriend."

"I know. I just don't know what to call him."

I ruffled Logan's hair. "I'll let you figure that one out then. But yes, he's staying tonight. We're watching films and he promised he would make tea just how you like it."

The game was brutal. Both Wales and Scotland played dirty at times and I could tell that the ref was getting frustrated with the amount of dirty tackles and rough play. But Rhys was like a knife on the field, slicing through every attempt the

Scottish players made to take him out. When Wales won by a comfortable enough margin to ensure Scotland would find it difficult to recover the rest of the tournament, I tried my best not to look too elated. My man was the best fucking player out there. And he was shooting for the stars.

The only disappointment in our relationship was the distance. Sarah and I were sharing the kids every other week now, and Rhys wasn't getting any time off rugby at all. So I was travelling from Edinburgh to Cardiff most weeks, except for the rare weekend, maybe twice or three times in a year, where Rhys would be playing near Edinburgh. But we were making the distance work, and he was staying over tonight for a quiet movie night, as it was my weekend with the kids. I couldn't wait.

We filtered from the stadium, Finn uttering a quick goodbye before heading over to the changing rooms to meet with Garrett and Wesley. I wasn't sure if there was something he was avoiding telling us, but that was Finn all over. He'd withdrawn himself little bit since his big scandal, and it made me sad to see.

***

Rhys

"How're my favourite kids?" I asked as Logan and Olivia ran toward me, their father just behind. Logan ran full force and smacked into my legs and Olivia caught herself before she got to me and held out a hand to shake. Thirteen year olds were weird.

"Got this for you," I said to her. I grabbed the rugby ball from my bag that had been signed by the Cardiff and Edinburgh players. "I know you're a fan, so…"

Olivia closed the distance and hugged me, ignoring the

squeals of her brother who was trapped between us. "Thanks," she said.

"No problem."

"That was really nice of you," said Callum. His beautiful deep Scottish voice felt like home, and I knew that my recent big decision was the right one. Not that Callum knew about or had agreed to it. But he would.

"We heading home, then?" he asked. Callum took my hand and let the kids lead the way to his flat, not far from the rugby field.

My heart was beating at a million miles an hour. Did I tell him now? Was it worth breaking the fragile peace? Or did I wait for the kids to go to bed? Or…

"I'mmovingtoEdinburghnextseason," I let out in one breath.

"What was that?" Callum asked, though I suspected he knew what I'd said and needed confirmation.

"I'm…I'm moving to Edinburgh in the new year," I said. "If you want me to. I won't come up if you're happy with the distance as it is, or I can find my own flat if you think it's too soon to move in together…but I'd like to give a proper go of this."

"But what about Cardiff?" Callum blurted. "Wait, no, that came out wrong. I'm thrilled that you want to move to Edinburgh, but…are you sure? Cardiff raised you."

"I've spoken to Garrett," I said. "Nothing stopping me for playing for Wales if I keep playing well for Edinburgh. But they've been scouting, and gave me a very good pay offer when I hinted I'd be willing to make the move. To be closer to you. To close that distance. If you want, though. If you don't want me to-"

"I. Am. Fucking. Thrilled." Callum stopped me in the middle

of the street to grab my face and kiss me — just quickly, before he had to let me go to keep an eye out for the kids several steps ahead of us. "You want to move in with me, right? No point buying a place up here when you'll be spending every night with me anyway."

I could feel myself blushing as I often did around Callum. "Yes. That sounds good to me...though I've got goldfish who need a place to stay too."

And we walked, hand in hand, to his little flat, where we cuddled up on the sofa and watched crap Disney films all night with the kids. I was home. And always would be.

***

A message from Matt...

Thanks so much for reading Pitch Prince! I hope you enjoyed, and I hope you'll continue to enjoy the series. If you did like the book, please leave a rating or review on Amazon or Goodreads. As a small author in a big pond, my books thrive when they get reviewed.

Next up we have *Lord of the Lock*. Finn deserves a happy ever after after all he's been through and he'll be finding it with a side character from my *West Wales Romance Series,* so if you've not read those books already why not check them out? *Available to pre-order now.*

Finally, I have a free serial featuring Garrett and Bernie, Cardiff's coach and physio, available to my newsletter subscribers. So if you want more of this series, you can head to the QR code below to pick it up or head to https://dl.bookfunnel.com/wpsrlh310d.

PITCH PRINCE

***

26

Sneak Peek - Book 2

Lord of the Lock (working title) is out on the 1st of June 2023. (if you're reading after then, you're in luck!) but here's a little sneak peak of what's to some. At first, I wasn't sure how this series would continue. But then Finn jumped out at me and forced me to write his novel, and an obscure side character from my last series finally had a story that would fit.

Finn

You're pathetic. My own internal voice was stronger almost than my external one. I'd always been a king in my own little domain, joker extraordinaire and centre of attention. I used my larger than life personality to mask the pain inside. I had partied hard, fucked relentlessly and completely screwed up my whole life in the process. And rock bottom was where I'd ended up.

Rock bottom in this case was the small welsh village of Pontycae, known as *Pont* unaffectionately by locals and visitors alike. Not that there were many visitors to Pont. It was a shithole, after all. It was where I'd chosen to start my self-exile after a couple of embarrassing missteps that had trashed my reputation in the world of rugby.

When I'd exiled myself I imagined that a quick call to the coach of my old team, Cardiff Old Navy, would have me reinstated and back on the payroll. But Garrett had moved on to coaching Wales and the new coach wasn't exactly keen to give up a place on his starting squad to someone with a reputation for derailing away trips and getting embarrassingly drunk at every opportunity. Not exactly star athlete material.

I gathered up bottles from the living room and passed through the kitchen to throw them into the rubbish bin outside. I had opened all the windows and the back door so that I could cover up the smell of alcohol that seemed to permeate everywhere. My best friends were coming round to check on me and I was determined that they see I was doing better. Even if I wasn't, exactly.

I sprayed a generous amount of Febreze around the room and made sure the little sofa was tidied up and tables wiped down. Now that the house didn't look like a homeless squat inhabited by angry alcoholics, it wasn't so bad.

At exactly 1pm there was a knock at the door, and I headed to open it with my heart in my mouth. Outside was a grinning Rhys Prince and his ridiculously well-styled Daddy of a boyfriend, Callum.

"How goes the day, Mr Anderson?" I asked as the big Scotsman pulled me in for a hug. Callum was one of the few people on a rugby field who almost looked eye-to eye with me. But I was still a couple inches taller than him. "Have you gained some weight?"

"Well not all of us are international rugby players any more," he said, ruffling Rhys' hair and then seeming to realise what he'd said. "Shit, I didn't mean...you'll be back to playing in no time."

"Sure," I snorted a laugh back, but his words had cut deep. If I hadn't been such an idiot then I would never have lost everything I held dear in life. But I was washed up at the age of twenty-seven and I had no idea how I'd dig myself out of the hole I was in.

"How's my favourite star?" I asked, grabbing Rhys and pulling him in for a bone-crushing hug to diffuse the tension in the room. "Score any tries against Scotland recently?"

"Enough," Rhys smirked, nudging Callum in the ribs.

"My nationalist heart lies with Scotland but my dick likes it when Wales win, what can I say," said Callum. "When Wales lose, I have to get the tissues out for an entirely different reason."

We all laughed, and it felt for a second like all the tension really had gone out of the room. We were just three old friends having a laugh, not two of the biggest legends in the game of rugby coming up to the arse-end of nowhere to console their washed up friend.

"Come on in," I said to the two of them, gesturing them into the living room. Not much had changed from when my grandparents had lived in the valley - the decor was still old-fashioned enough to be considered antique and the sofa was a squishy floral thing that I had never actually ascertained if my grandmother had died sitting in. Now she was six-foot under and my parents were living hundreds of miles away, I had no desire to find out.

"Tea? Coffee?" I asked. The only big changes anywhere in the house were all the fancy electronics I'd brought from

Cardiff. In the living room I had my top of the range games consoles and TV, and the kitchen was decked out with my smart-fridge, smart-washer and smart....well, everything really. All my appliances were connected to one another and to the internet in some way, which had been great in Cardiff where the WiFi was speedy. Here, things. Crashed more often than not.

"Alexa, three shots of espresso," I said. Thankfully, there was no delay and the coffee machine started to hum as it ground down the beans.

"We should get one of those," said Rhys as I brought the coffees in. "They're well cool."

"Around my kids? They'd be ordering more than I could afford as soon as they figured out how to use the thing," Callum laughed.

"Tell them their Uncle Finn misses them," I said. I had a soft spot for Logan and Olivia. They were sweet kids and Callum was nice enough to let me around them when lots of people were wary because of my past stupidity. I did my best not to be too bad an influence on them.

"They miss their Uncle Finn too," said Callum. "How's living back up here? Any good local pubs?"

"Callum," Rhys warned in the least subtle tone I'd ever heard.

"Seriously Rhys, you don't have to walk on eggshells around me. I can go for the odd pint without being a complete loon," I lied. As far as he knew, I was getting a real handle on any alcohol dependencies. So long as he didn't hear my bins rattling with the sound of bottles everything was fine.

"Well in that case, fancy going out for a meal?" he asked. I groaned internally. I *could* do it.

"Go on then, let's find a pub in this shithole," I said.

***

The Eagle was rough, but they did a good burger. At least that's how I justified it as Rhys and Callum followed me in and Rhys' eyes widened at the sight. The old place hadn't been updated since about 1973 and the tables were never as clean as they could be. Despite it being only 1pm, there were a couple of local alcoholics in the corner already off their face on Special Brew and who knew what else.

"Morning," one said to me with a little too much familiarity, and I nodded briefly before dragging Rhys and Callum over to a table in the corner.

"Stop staring like you're on a foreign excursion," I said to Rhys. "This isn't the third world."

"Sorry, I just…"

"Surely you've played rugby in some rough places?" I asked.

Callum chuckled. "I remember when I was amateur and we played a match in Glasgow that ended after ten minutes because of player fighting. That was *rough*, but it was fun."

I remembered then that Rhys, despite only being a couple years younger than me and almost a decade younger than his boyfriend, hadn't come up through the amateur ranks in the same Valleys shitholes that I had, or the places in Scotland that likely looked very similar to where we were sat.

"I'll get you both a drink. Pint?" I asked. "Don't look at me like that, Rhys. I can have a pint and not relapse."

Never mind that the relapse had already happened. I headed to the bar and ordered three pints off the grizzled old bartender who had been behind the bar back when my friends and I had started drinking at thirteen.

I brought our pints over and set them down in front of Rhys

and Callum. "What's on the menu, then?" Rhys asked.

"Burgers," I replied. He really was too precious for this place.

"What kind of burgers? I love burger places."

I pointed to the scrawled whiteboard at the back of the bar. "Well you can have a burger, or a cheeseburger. If you ask nicely you might even get some sauce."

"Oh." Rhys looked back down at his pint and his cheeks turned red. There was a pub down the road that offered nicer fare, but it was always packed out as the only decent place in town to get a meal. Every date night, wedding party and birthday took place at the Post Hotel down the road.

Callum slipped his arm around Rhys, unconcerned at where we were, and kissed him on the top of his head. "Seems that rugby being a man's sport died back when I was making my way up through the ranks, eh. All on silver platters now…"

"Piss off," Rhys replied. "One of us has retired to nice comfy commentary boxes, and one of us still gets down and dirty in the mud. I wonder if you can figure out who…"

I laughed along with them both and looked around the pub again. The place never changed, and neither did the people. Which is why I was so taken aback when a shock of hot-pink hair entered the room.

The bright pink was attached to a little man, surely at least a foot shorter than me and skinny. He was dressed in matching denim shirt and jeans and was wearing too-big round glasses. He was frowning as his eyes darted around the room, like a herbivore checking a field for predators before darting across. He held the door open for an older man in a wheelchair I vaguely recognised and then they both headed to a table in the very far corner of the room, ages away from anyone else.

"Hello, Earth to Finn?" Rhys waved a hand in front of my

face and brought me back to our table. "Something caught your eye?" he smirked.

"Nothing," I muttered. "Anyway. Burger. Cheese. Sauce?"

"I'll get these," said Callum, standing up. "I know what you both like." He walked over to the bar with his empty pint glass to order.

"And I know you like a twink," Rhys muttered. "Do you and that guy know each other?"

I looked over to where the guy was stood at the bar. Something in my mind was firing up at the sight of him, but I had no idea if it was recognition, arousal or both. I knew most people in this town, so it was weird that I couldn't quite place him. Especially with his bright pink hair.

He was ordering at the bar but even then his eyes were darting around the room like he was scared of something. He seemed to instinctively lean away from Callum and his bulk, and he walked quickly back to his table as soon as he'd been served his pint and a glass of water.

"Bloody hell Finn, stop looking and answer my bloody question," Rhys said.

What question? Oh, yeah. "I don't know him," I said. "Though I really should…"

"Thought you were swearing off hookups whilst you were here?"

"I am, I just mean…everyone knows everyone around here. And there's only one high school in the village, so I'm sure I should know him…"

"Bloody hell, £1 a burger," Callum interrupted. "And £3 a pint! We should come here more often."

"We really should *not*," Rhys said, and I had to agree with him. It was nice to have the two of them around but it messed with my ability to wallow in peace. A tiny little part of me wanted to be around the table with the old alcoholics and to drink myself into a stupor. Instead I forced myself to drink my pint at a glacial pace as Callum finished off a second and third and Rhys had a second. I had to prove to them I was in some kind of control.

The door to the pub opened and I heard the familiar laughter and voices of a couple of the lads from the local grassroots rugby team. Like most people around here, they had grown up in the town and had gone to the same high school, joined a rugby team and worked in similar trades. I forgot their names, as they'd played for Pandy rugby team whilst I'd played for the semi-professional Pont. Those of us who were lucky enough had gotten out in the end, gone on to bigger and better things. Maybe I was even unluckier for having come back.

Both their voices stopped abruptly and I looked up. I thought they might have spotted the three international rugby stars in their midst but they weren't looking at us at all. They were looking at the pink-haired man in the corner. And his fear looked like it had been ratcheted up to a whole new level.

The second they took a step towards him, I was up on my feet and ready to fight.

Available to pre-order via Amazon now. Coming June 2023.

Acknowledgements

Thank you to Bella Lucas for beta-ing for me, I don't think you'll ever realise how insanely helpful you are or how I wish our friendship wasn't separated by the Atlantic Ocean.

Thank you to Jack, my fiance, for always, always inspiring me to write love stories about impossibly gorgeous and brilliant men. You are sweeter than any romantic hero, and the most gorgeous rugby player I know.

And thank you to you, dear reader, for taking a chance on this book. I really hope you enjoyed, and I hope you stick around for more Rucking Rugby Men.

Also by Matt Peters

Handy Man (West Wales Romance, Book 1)

James is forced to escape his home city of London after a mugging leaves him shaken. He finds solace in the picturesque seaside village of Hiraeth, where he meets Llywelyn, a rugged and charming handyman who turns James' world upside down. Despite only having a week to spend in Hiraeth, their feelings for one another deepen. How will James reconcile his life in the city with his new feelings for country boy Llywelyn?

Hollywood Crush (West Wales Romance, Book 2)

When B-list actor Daniel Ellison is cast in a big-budget fantasy TV series filming in the seaside village of Hiraeth, he's not exactly thrilled. But when he meets Tudor, the charming and determined hotelier, their initial animosity quickly turns to passion. As they navigate their opposing lifestyles and the challenges of filming in a small town, they soon realize they have more in common than they thought.

Full Service (West Wales Romance, Book 3)

Hywel Prentis returns to the Welsh seaside village of Hiraeth, after his partner in life and in business cheats him out of his hard-earned money. As he adjusts to life back in his hometown, he's forced to confront his troubled past with his ex-best friend's younger brother, Macsen. Macsen, the town mechanic, is not the same boy Hywel left behind and as they work to repair old wounds, they can no longer ignore the spark of attraction between them.